Praise for Paul D Blumer's
Death or Quarter

In Paulie Gaeta—bare-knuckled boxer, arrogant Boston underdog, proud father, violent dreamer, quiet reader, closet mystic, petty street hustler, and long-term prison inmate #30583-012—debut novelist Paul Blumer has conjured up a notable trickster-narrator. Artfully served up, this story of youth and age, time and eternity, sways sharply between hard-edged, vernacular and bold, shape-shifter storytelling. As convicted Paulie relives, reweaves and recasts his wayward tale, readers may tease out the devil from the details. They may also unearth the world, the flesh and rushes of dream-spirit. Paul Blumer has penned an exciting first novel.

—*Al Young, poet-novelist-essayist*
and California's ex-poet laureate

Death or Quarter

ooooo

a novel

by Paul D Blumer

Death or Quarter is dedicated to Jen and Ed, without whom it would be a hollow tale indeed.

And for my parents, who mostly encouraged, or at least tolerated the tomfoolery from a young age.

Acknowledgements and a thousand thanks to:

John Rubadeau, whose indelible teachings have followed me through the days of my life. His language-intricate philosophy, boiled down to *Scratch your itch,* has doubtless influenced and saved hundreds, if not thousands, of proud Ann Arbor championites.

My lovely lady of the lake—er, Brooke—without whose adoring sustenance I would have long-since perished, leaving behind just a scattering of words in the breeze.

All my willing Readers, with a good balance of praise and criticism—you know who you are. Without you this would be choppy and incomplete.

The CCA grad-writing faculty, for their openness to and excitement for new voices, new work, and new ideas.

My family members who never hesitate to show me the other side of the looking glass.

Ed G; if you've found your way into a copy, give me a call. You have my number.

The giants on whose shoulders I stand: the view is priceless.

And all the naysayers who've galvanized my stubborn pen.

Inspired by true stories.

Our dried voices, when
We whisper together
Are quiet and meaningless

T.S. Eliot "The Hollow Men"

Your mind goes blank.

Pop! Like that moment during an orgasm or yawn. That one instant when everything shuts down, leaving an empty chassis. Higher consciousness forfeit, senses unfiltered. Time and place forgotten.

You notice the world rising all around.

You're falling.

For that one instant, you are falling. Flash vision of that fall continuing all the way to the dust that will soon become your permanent residence.

But then your knees catch—instinct takes over, and you duck the next punch. Adrenaline floods gut-chest-neck-eyes-mind, sucking away pain and pumping in rage. An animal takes charge.

Raw reaction and a surge of calm violence. Control.

Squinting at my opponent behind a wall of forearms, I twist my head and crack my neck. Gotta roll with the punches.

The first hit in any fight is the best. You build up this anticipation thinking about the fight, imagining worst-case scenario after worst-case scenario, picturing that jaw-breaking first blow.

But when the knuckles connect, it's never as bad as you expected. Training and toughness. Recognition and experience. The rest of this will be a breeze.

And now I make this man pay.

Luis Corpus. Squared off, wary of retaliation and looking for openings. A born fighter—quick, and more or less wiry for this event. Six-seven, two-forty, tattooed and scarred like nobody's business. Prison ink. He's the Peruvian favorite, brought in from Lima by some of my...associates.

Associates whose names I don't even want to know, guys involved in business networks with fingers in pies of all kinds, these corporations wielding so much raw power and money, that few even know they exist. Who else would organize illegal bare-knuckle fights?

The bets are flying thick and heavy, and everyone is serious. For the spectators, it's serious cash. For the Feds, it's serious felony. For us—for me and this man Luis—it's serious life and death.

And each player thinks his own serious is the most important.

Head bobbing, nostrils flared. Squared-off and circling. Smelling blood, and thirsty. Luis Corpus. A dead man.

There's a reason I'm facing this man I don't know, this Peruvian kid wearing creased-new Carhartts and a pair of Timberlands so fresh, the leather is still unburnished over the steel toes. There's a reason I'm bare-chested and carved like granite. There's a reason my nose is bleeding and broken flat.

And there's a reason I don't give a shit.

We're all in it for the same reason, however many zeros come after it. At the very basic, it's a thing of survival, of continuing to thrive, of adapting to the environment and amassing as much of its fruit as possible. The instinct to possess, to maintain a foothold in this slippery world—to ensure tomorrow.

There's a world full of things people would do for money. Who among us can say he's never done anything other than right, for the almighty dollar? That guy can throw the first stone.

And then I'm gonna throw it right back, straight at his head.

Money.

Money makes the world go round. Money grows on trees—if you own the trees. Money makes men do a lot of things. Money makes me fight—well, money plus a ferocious impulse to win.

There's a lot I wouldn't do for ten grand, but punching the shit out of some other juiced-up gorilla for the pleasure of a bunch of drug lords and tycoons doesn't bother me. Hell, I'd do it for free.

But I don't. I'm paid and honor-bound, contracted and enthralled. Life signed away. Might as well have been my blood in that fountain pen long ago. My blood is in the fight as much as the fight is in my blood.

So here I am.

Winner gets ten thousand. *I* get ten thousand.

Loser gets two grand. You want to see me fight, you have to have a million cash, just to get in. From there it's side bets worth more than my car, on every little aspect of the fight. Hundred large on someone calling mercy; quarter million on whether a guy gets up from a stumble. Fifty grand on over/under number of punches landed.

I'm a valuable champion, but don't be fooled: these guys couldn't care less about me, and I don't give a shit about them, as long as they don't ever try to get me to take a fall for cash. That day happens, if one of these cologne-soaked glass-jaw gangsters ever offers to buy the outcome of a fight, if a slickie crook ever asks me to go down after five punches, that day I quit. That day I quit by taking his wide colorful tie and adjusting it three or four inches.

Here's a secret: pride is the only thing worth more than money...you just can't buy anything with it.

Here's another secret: it's also the real reason I fight. I can make more cash in other ways. But there's no better way to get that feeling, that thrill when you walk out and start circling, measuring up the opponent, and it's just you and him, life and death. There's no other way to make thirty spectators disappear than to face off one-on-one in a game that might leave one of us dead. There is no drug that can compare.

Believe it or not I'd rather fight a guy taller than me. Truth. Against a taller fighter, you throw uppercuts and high-explosive jawbreakers. You drop in under his guard, and right there at eye level is the soft throat. When you fight a big guy, it's all he can do to swing downwards, exposing himself to devastating blows to the chin with each level drop. This isn't boxing.

No, it's the little dudes you have to watch out for, the little Bruce Lee roosters who dodge in and out, ducking right under your punches. And God forbid you ever lose to someone smaller than you. Can't let the underdog take away the bone.

This guy, this Luis Corpus, thinks his wingspan and height give him the edge. It's making him cocky—that or he's just got a sloppy, lanky style. Either way, I'm seeing openings.

He's getting careless, throwing haymakers that I easily dodge. He's grown up fighting in prison, where fights are haphazard at best, a matter of wild swinging in hopes of landing some ferocious hits before you take a nightstick to the belly. His style is like using a Mac-10: spray 'n' pray. I've got conditioning and experience on my side.

His chest is heaving, shining with Vaseline and sweat. I can rope-a-dope this guy until he makes a crucial mistake. Just a matter of time...

You don't see a guy's eyes much in a fight. The eyes lie. There's a point in space somewhere around his mid torso and a few inches in front of his chest. That's where you focus. Maximize the field of peripherals, brain concentrating on the whole picture. Motion-sensor mode.

Timing is everything.

He drops a hand to hitch his dungarees, and I dive in with a glancing cross. He stumbles back and shakes it off, blowing a mist of spit and blood before shrugging and returning to his guard. His lips glisten scarlet and tremble slightly as he breathes.

We circle, bouncing on toes in the dust, never still.

Stop moving for one second in this sport, and next thing you know, you're on the ground, and a steel-toe boot is making a hole in your head.

Footwork is essential, and the hours spent hopping over a jump-rope pay off in the end. I don't want to have to think about my feet.

So we circle, bouncing on toes, glaring between uplifted fists in search of openings.

Jab.

Jab.

Tentative. Lunge and jab, lunge and back again.

Left foot forward, right leg flexed like a coiled spring. Round and round.

Get the fuck to it, cabrón! someone shrieks from outside the ring.

And then I get hit.

I'm on my back, rolling away from Corpus' boots and trying to shake the stars out of my eyes and the ringing from my ears. He seems surprised that I'm down, and I take advantage of his hesitation to scramble back and get on my feet again. Distraction is part of the game, and this time it caught me off-guard. If Luis Corpus had been more experienced or more driven, I'd be a dead man.

A fight is a dance. Shuffle back, bob and weave, bouncing toes, back and back, back back and *BANG!* Lure the motherfucker in and make him pay. Pinpoint punches—hard!—jaw, ear, break the nose, smash the collarbone.

There's a technique and a reason for everything.

It's not chaos.

It's choreography versus choreography. If I can break this guy's nose, his eyes will water, no matter how tough he is. Then I'm attacking a blind man fighting through a blur. If I can snap his collarbone, he's minus a weapon; minus a shield. If I can scare him enough about my ability to deliver pain, he'll make a mistake, and then I'm in.

There's a hole in the ground waiting for him if I catch him just right.

It's a funny thing about this bare-knuckle death circuit that rotates among a scattering of secluded ranches owned by a file cabinet somewhere. You try it out and it's kinda scary, kind of exciting, like skydiving or racing cars. You're jacked on adrenaline, and it hurts like a motherfucker sometimes, and you're constantly aching: permanent black eyes, throbbing knuckles, cauliflower ear—the works. But it's also addictive like no drug I've ever tried. You get the feeling that you can wreck absolutely anybody, and you cannot wait to start hitting.

I walk through the supermarket, and I want to punch that guy in the Gold's Gym t-shirt just for standing in front of the protein powder I want to buy. I want to slap the bartender for overfilling my glass and spilling beer. I want to pick fights with two, three, four guys at a time. I want to fight fight *fight*. Nobody can fuck with me, but I *have* to find someone with the grit to take me on toe to toe, someone who can actually stand against me. There's an instinct we all have, no matter how deeply buried, to find the alpha and bring him down by any means available, to dominate no matter what. Ask Darwin. Ask Brezhnev. Ask the President.

Call me an animal. I agree. We're *all* animals, kept in line by a set of social standards and hereditary habits.

And as an animal, I'm absorbed by an evolutionary need to win win win, to prove my progenitive prowess time and time again—to keep partaking of the sweet juicy fruits of the world. *My* world.

And to do that, I need a challenge. A *challenge*. Not this guy. He's just a kid I'm going to demolish.

Luis Corpus. He advances as I swipe a fist across my lips. The stinging pain galvanizes my body, and I leap toward him, juking right and swinging a left-hook *pap!* directly into his temple as he bobs away from the feint.

His arms drop, his eyes glaze over, and he falls like a cardboard cutout in a puff of chalky dust. My left arm vibrates with pain, radiating all through my elbow and into my shoulder.

I can smell the blood dripping from my split knuckles, and I step back to watch the kid.

He doesn't move.

It's over.

I turn away, and my body sags in the adrenal aftermath. A metallic taste, like sucking pennies, on my tongue. I collect the purse and walk away, past the waiting backhoe, past the food-laden tables, toward a shower, not bothering to see if Corpus gets up. If he does, he'll be sent packing. The loser isn't invited to the after-party.

A wrecked car sits at the edge of a grove of trees, still smoking from the weapons demonstration before the fight. Long ago, after one of my earlier bouts, I bought a concealable Walther PPK to carry around, after watching the arms dealer with a semiautomatic SPAS-12 shotgun rip apart a taxi in seconds. In another show, I'd nearly gone deaf from the concussion of an RPG. And a demo of an AK-47 mod once made me worry about the plight of Democracy. But now, it's sort of just a pissing match. I don't even want to know who's buying what weapons.

At this ranch, where you drive from the highway about six hours up the driveway before you get to the main house, there's an ominous presence of power. You can feel it prickling the hair on your neck, tingling the skin under your balls, dancing at the back of your throat. This is the kind of place where you're on your best behavior.

Despite that, I'm leaving before the party, as soon as I get my suit on. I have to get back to Boston. There are thirty keys of the finest snow stashed in a couple of duffels in the locker room of the gym I'm now the sole owner of, since Alonzo's demise, and I'd hate for it to melt in the summer heat.

ooooo

I grew up like any other American kid. School, chores, cartoons, working-class parents. Except I was short and fat, and had nothing to say to any number of bullies who slouched around the housing project where my parents had been inconsiderate enough to raise me.

My life was basically laid out and hopeless. No matter how good my grades were, I could never afford college. I was set to become a janitor or handyman or mechanic, and my best bet was to get a job working in some nice neighborhood outside the city, where I'd maybe stand to make a decent enough wage to put a down payment on some shitty house and live in debt the rest of my miserable life, raising my own slum kids and riding the hamster wheel of the American Dream.

There was an image I had—a dream sometimes—of myself sitting in a kitchen nodding into a newspaper, pushing reading glasses up my nose every ten seconds, cup of coffee growing cool on a Formica tabletop. I'd wake up from the dream in a cold sweat, clueless as to what had freaked me out, until I went into the kitchen for breakfast, and saw my pops, drowsing into a bowl of soup next to his newspaper, still wearing his nightshift uniform with its aluminum flashlight and laminated badge.

As soon as anyone discovered my father was an LBJ-worshipping rent-a-cop, I became a target. I was used to it. I had a half a dozen spots around the project grounds where I'd scuttle and hide when someone was after my yo-yo or lunch pail or whatever. I kept mostly to myself, avoiding the playground and other kids, reading library books, and swiping candy bars from newsstands when I could. It was a rat's existence, and I look back on it with disgust, but at the time I didn't know any better. There was only one way to pull myself out for real.

I had to get involved in something.

When you have almost nothing, the one frivolous thing you own can mean the world. It can mean a peek into another existence, where money is just part of getting dressed.

One year for Christmas and my eleventh birthday combined, my folks managed to scrape a few extra dollars to buy me a fancy new sled. I remember unwrapping the thing and dancing around the mudroom-sized family room like a chubby little gnome, feeling like a king. That little red sled was my be-all and end-all, with its razor-sharp runners and a brand-new manila rope knotted through the wood alongside the words *Flexible Flyer*. Pure magic. I wanted to ride that thing every minute of every day, until everything else sort of faded away.

Enter Mikey Stone, the ugly pimp who supervised the project, terrorizing the hundreds of resident families and swaggering around at the head of his little band like the Sheriff of Nottingham.

The son or nephew or cousin of someone with enough influence to get him the position, Mikey Stone regularly rifled through people's mail and purposely lost rent checks to collect late fees. Nobody ever did anything about it. We all lived in fear. I avoided him and his gang at all costs.

The original founders would be disgusted to see what their Welcome-Home-Heroes-V-E-Day Housing Project had rotted into after all the vets had made their way up in the world and moved out to the suburbs.

It was a Tuesday, I remember. Everyone was still talking about Max McGee's unlikely performance in the NFL Championship over the weekend. I'd cut school to play on the sled, bumping down ice-slick steps in front of the building under the kind of blue sky that makes you wonder if maybe everything will work out after all. I was lugging the sled back up the measly hill, when Mikey Stone and his four goons hopped out of a Twinkie-colored Plymouth Duster, and sauntered over.

"That's a wicked-nice sled, kid," whistled Mikey. His companions sniggered and pawed at each other, closing a circle around me. I nodded and kept my eyes on the ground, hoping they'd just go away.

"Kin I try it?" He reached out a hand and flipped it a couple times, *gimme gimme*. I looked up.

His eyes were droopy and yellow. A jaundiced undershirt peeped out from his low-zipped Red Sox jacket, half hiding a silver chain winking in the sun. I hugged the sled and shook my head silently, wiping my nose on a mitten knit by some auntie.

"No?" Mikey was incredulous. "Did he just say *no*, boys?" They nodded and laughed.

Uh oh.

He stepped toward me, glaring down and wagging a finger in my face.

"Listen to me, you little motherfucker," he growled, with breath that would wilt sawgrass, "I *was* gonna take it for a ride, but now I'm just gonna *take* it. Give it here."

I shook my head.

Get bent, bully, I imagined screaming. I saw myself lifting the sled over my head and swinging it with inhuman strength directly into his fat purple night-crawler lips, standing over him and chopping the edge toward his neck like a guillotine again and again. Then—even at eleven years old—I'd chase after his motley gang and clean the streets of a few more petty hoods.

Holy dreaming doofus, Batman.

Instead, I just tightened my grip on the sled while Mikey and his thugs sneered and reached for it.

Suddenly I was down, staring at the powder-blue sky through a drifting galaxy of yellow sparks. Ears ringing. Temples throbbing.

I hadn't even seen the fist coming.

Hot coppery blood slid down my throat, and I gagged, tears brimming in my eyes. My face burned. The thugs laughed.

My hands were empty—they'd torn the sled out of my grip and were passing it around the circle over my head. *I will not cry. I will not give them the satisfaction. I will not let these rats get to me.*

They grabbed my arms. Two of them sat on my legs. Mikey stooped and unzipped my coat. He dug in a pocket and popped a switchblade. Then he grabbed a handful of my shirt and snarled with murder in his eyes, "Don't you ever say no to me, boy. Not if you value your shitty little life." He slit my shirt and pulled it open, exposing my chest.

"Here's a little lesson, punk," he said. "This is *my* turf. Anything on it belong to *me*." Then he dropped trou and squatted. I watched his asshole twitch once or twice, and then it bulged slightly and peeled slowly back around a glistening brown torpedo, stretching thin and squelching softly. Underneath, his nuts quivered. Then the shit thumped hot on my chest.

"Including you."

The thugs ran off.

I sat up and spat blood. The turd clung for a second before tumbling into my lap, leaving streaks on my stomach as I watched them skip and hoot, honking the horn as the Duster skidded down the road.

I broke a tooth grinding my jaw.

ooooo

Believe it or not, I moved on. No sense wallowing. When you're a slug, you can't do anything against the folks who come pluck you up and fling you around for sport, and so you get used to the abuse and learn to take it with a grain of salt—which makes it that much worse for the slug.

The following fall, newly twelve, I took a job as an assistant janitor at an apartment complex on the Fenway.

How expected.

My job was to run around with a nail-embedded broom handle, spearing bits of garbage, which I did for a whole year before graduating to gathering the piles of filled trash bags around the grounds, hauling them to a pickup which carried them to the dump.

After another year of that, they finally told me that I'd be driving the truck once I got my license at sixteen. And I was supposed to be grateful and proud. More pennies and more respect in the custodial world.

Instead I was thinking, two more years of this? Maybe just kill me now.

But that was the job. There was nothing I could do about my life without some savings. So I plugged on, and pretended to be optimistic about the labor.

Now and then an illegal Mexican—or Salvadoran or Puerto Rican or whatever—would hitch a ride in the garbage truck and stick around to work on some painting or laying new linoleum to replace squares loosened to hide junkie stashes. They'd probably make more money if they went around ripping up the rest of floor, selling whatever treasures they found buried there, but somehow they're too honest.

I didn't know any Spanish, and I never much trusted anyone anyway, so they were all just faceless migrant workers. Which meant I thought nothing of it when one day the truck pulled up with a dude in a sweatshirt sitting in the bed.

I was carrying four trashbags, holding them with arms straight out, loving the way my sweatshirt stretched taut against my trembling muscles, and how the cotton pulled against the five or eight chest hairs I'd been cultivating. For months I'd been making a game out of work, hoisting the trashbags like dumbbells, and after enough hours of such work, muscles turn to cables, and skin turns to leather. I felt the job turning me into something hard and functional, and I liked that.

Since the day I lost my sled, I'd been ripping pushups at a rate of dozens a day, trying to push out the memory-burned image of Mikey Stone by focusing my anger and exhausting my rage. I was sick of being the fat kid, the quiet acquiescing victim of any bully. A growth spurt this summer had left me bigger than a lot of the other fourteen-year-olds and I worked to stay on top of that. Never again would I face the humiliation and disgrace of bowing before a power greater than my own.

I couldn't afford a weight set, but I had scooped a weight bench from a garage sale. With a bag of concrete from the construction site down the block and some buckets, I made barbells with a pair of mop handles. I spent all my free time in the maintenance shed on that cracked vinyl, relishing the *shhh* of my sweaty back peeling off as I sat up, breathing in the cold machine smell. I dreamt in rhythmic clinking, and took bodybuilder books from the library to improve my technique.

As the calluses on my palms grew, my anger hardened into something calm and virulent, and I tucked it into the pit of my stomach where it sat and waited. I could feel it behind my bellybutton when I looked in the mirror, finally approving of the scowling figure I saw there.

I could feel it when I mumbled *Yes sir, no sir* to my bosses.

I could feel it when Grandpa, in a rare moment of vigor and clarity, scolded and slapped me for letting my grades slip. *That ain't my problem, it's yours. But you GET your GRADES back UP.*

I could feel it when I played King of the Hill with neighborhood kids until my knees were oozing and bubbly with filthy scrapes, and I was finally standing alone on the top.

I could feel it all the time.

It had been ages since Mikey Stone had left the projects for grimier pastures, but I still thought about him every day as I let my anger use my body to push its muscles past the point of pain.

I thought about wrapping my arm around his throat, and cranked a few more curls.

I thought about shoving him through windows, and pushed a few more presses.

I thought about stomping his face under my workboots, and gritted out a few more squats.

Between lifting weights and work, I kept myself distracted and mostly out of trouble, but I began feeling a powerful wanderlust. There was no way I could stomach this minimum-wage job much longer. I needed to get out of the projects and into the world—even if that meant something like loan sharking.

"Hey, Paulie, this guy's here to meet the new manager about a job."

I nodded and barely glanced up, thinking mostly about my count. Forty-five...forty-six...forty-seven...

My record was a minute with four full bags outstretched. But something familiar about the guy made me stop and look again. Those lips flapping in the breeze, the hint of a sneer hooking his wide nose, the thick low forehead. I froze.

Mikey Stone. With no goons.

I dropped the bags and lunged toward the truck which had brought me such a nice gift. I leapt up on the tailgate and grabbed him by the collar. His surprise changed to fear as I wrenched him toward the edge. He recognized me.

"Remember me, motherfucker?" I hissed. I hopped down from the truck, pulling Mikey along by the sweatshirt—then I yanked him off and rocked my leg up, slapping his face around my knee like a pumpkin. He collapsed and sprawled unmoving for a moment, and I stood waiting. He pulled himself to his knees and stood woozily, reaching in his pocket for a knife.

No way. It's *my* turn now. And I'm on him, throwing my entire weight behind a right cross which connects CRACK on his chin. He stumbles back, and I swing around with my left, smashing my fist into his temple. He drops to the sidewalk. The switchblade clatters across the pavement. I'm on him, fists flailing, red mist rising before my eyes DIE *you fucking worm piece of shit*; my fist again and again socking wet and hard into his ugly brown face, drawing back and throwing myself down again and again, fists elbows fist fist *fist* blood spraying teeth bared screaming venting MOTHER-FUCKER *die!* as the accumulation of my hatred toward him boils over, and all the anger of feeling helpless takes control, CHOCK chock thuck tap thap DIE the back of his head cracks and spills red on the pavement, wide wet eyes cross lose focus, arms fall to the draw of gravity as his body gives up, and still I'm on him thrashing and flailing and *mash*ing his face again and again with raw knuckles elbows bleeding breath ragged DIE DIE *DIE* as he goes limp beneath me, my knees soaked through with hot blood, heart thumping, fists pumping, rage shrieking, and spit flecking into his unseeing eyes, and his head cracking against the pavement with each savage blow; I'm on him *brap brap brap brap* as my fists take on a life of their own, lips splitting, teeth flying, tongue bitten through, skin torn and bruised, losing shape just a DIE mass of blood and cells and follicles of DIE a bully who chose the wrong victim with infinite patience and unceasing *hat*red.

I was panting and exhausted when I finally got up. The driver of the pickup stared agape, and I leveled a glare at him.

"The fuck you looking at?"

He shook his head and drove off. It was time for me to go.

ooooo

Lights on.

Morning.

"Gaeta! On your feet."

Time to be counted. Prisoner 30583-012 is still here.

"Your turn at the phone, right after breakfast."

All you can do is nod and try not to yawn.

A phone call's good. Breaks up the routine; gives you something to think about and anticipate. Even though a lot of times they just go wicked wrong, and you walk away feeling empty, pissed off, dissociative; there's nothing better than a taste of the outside world—like when the news went around that O.J. got acquitted and the homeboys all went nuts. A nibble of caviar in hell's food court. Good.

A yawn's bad. A yawn can get you in all sorts of stupid trouble, like *You bored or somethin'? Need to go back to bed instead of out to play? You mocking me, you little piss-ant? How about a nice trip to the SHU where no one can catch your yawn, faggot?* They always ask trap questions like that. Best to bite your tongue to keep from answering, or else pay the price for whatever smart-ass words come out. Bad.

Avoid trouble. Keep to yourself.

They say every criminal winds up in the slammer. Honestly, you can't bitch and moan too much about it. If you're all kinds of crook and you're stupid enough to get caught, you go to jail. That's the game.

Years of brawls and assaults, years of loan sharking, years of illegal prize fights that sometimes end in death, and the judgment they finally level is twenty-four years for moving cocaine and Percocet through the gym, plus a handful of tax evasion and laundering charges. With gnarled knuckles soaked in blood, that kind of bid ain't so bad, given a little perspective.

Breakfast sucks.

How many days can you have the same off-gray cookie-cutter crap before you turn into a forty-year-old jellyfish? Some guys deal with it by stealing fruit and fermenting it with sugar into pruno. Then they show up hammered, and meals are magically transformed into something palatable.

Either way, you eat the whole goddamn mess because it's all there is. Pretty soon you forget there's anything else. You forget the lobster-tail. You forget the 18-ounce porterhouses. You forget the crabcakes and gravy and barbecued ribs. Forget all that.

You eat, because otherwise your muscle melts away. Skin hangs in folds. Nails crack. Teeth loosen. Lips split. You eat because if you don't, your status as a fighter is meaningless, and then you can't even defend yourself.

At this point you'd kill for a simple bowl of penne with garlic and olive oil.

Memories from the Outside mingle and run together with memories from the joint, until the whole string of personal history gets snarled and confusing.

Sometimes an old-timer will stand up and declare *I am not a crook!* as if the cheeky phrase were something new. Sometimes guys will wake up in the middle of the night begging a first-grade teacher not to kick them out of school. Sometimes a guy will demand answers: *Where the hell is Corbata?* forgetting that *compadre* died three years ago.

Present and past blur in a twisted clusterfuck, and whatever moment you are in, *now* is the lens for every aspect of every memory that comes to the surface.

This is the Big House. This is where guys get raped and stomped for being the little man, for being a piss-ant sucker bottom-feeder. There's few real friends. There's no permanent loyalty. There's only lights-on in the morning, lights-out at night, and might-makes-right in between. It's a life-and-death hierarchy here. Which makes it a perfect savage microcosm of the Outside. This is Hell's version of the real world.

You add capital letters to things inside your head, because that's the only place you're Free. That's the only place they can't inspect and toss. It's the only place where you can safely keep contraband.

So you nurture it.

Read books from the cart of donations.

Retreat.

You promise out what's left of your assets, and brownnose and cajole to get a cell without a cellie for as long as possible, and you study and read and correspond with a guy you know, and eventually earn a degree in philosophy from University of Phoenix. You embrace what's inside your head.

Because you can. Because you have to. Because you have nothing but Time. Nothing but a ceiling overhead to stare at and contemplate from every imaginable angle.

At some point even fantasizing about sex hour after hour can get boring.

"Gaeta! Get to the phones. Use it or lose it, chief."

Nod and say thank you, sir. Ignore the biting sarcasm of the address. Then shuffle off to the phonebank after handing your tray to a lackey, punch a number, and wait with the receiver pressed against your ear.

"Hello?"

This is how it goes.

"Hey, sweetheart, it's me."

"Me. Me who?" She sounds tired.

Smile. Always smile.

"There someone else calls you 'sweetheart'?"

Silence roars through the receiver.

"I'm just kiddin', babe, how are you?"

Make a stupid joke like that, expect to get burned. Say something dumb and eat your words. Swallow the bitter pride. Screaming into the phone gets privileges revoked. Or worse.

"Not bad. Good...I mean, I'm used to it, but it's not so pleasant, you know? At least I have Dante."

Yeah.

"Speaking of, he wants to ask you something. Here."

"Daddy?"

"Yeah, buddy, what's shakin'?"

"Daddy, can I go camping!"

"Of course you can, Dante. Put your mom back on."

"Hey."

"You planning on taking him? Can't get your nails done in a tent."

"Tex wants to take him."

"Tex? *Tex* does?"

ooooo

I asked for a throwaway.

Call me what you will, but it's my eightieth fight. And I've won them all. I don't even care to imagine how much money I've made for these fat cats, and the least they can do when I'm this close to fulfilling my contract is give me a pushover to mash up.

"Yeah, alright," said a suit whose name I'll never know. "You got it."

I was a little miffed at first when I saw the guy's pretty big, maybe six-three, two-eighty-five, but he's goofy-looking with a smushed potato of a nose sitting atop a mustache like a fat caterpillar carrying a sack.

And soft muscle tone. But bouncing around, shadow-boxing, loosening up.

Just like me.

Despite his unimpressive appearance, he looked tight and in control. But so does everyone, mostly. Until they get hit.

"You know," I said to the suit, "he looks kinda worrisome."

"Yeah, but look at him. Everybody's obviously hit him. Nose all over the place. That cauliflower ear."

"I guess you're right."

Bringing myself into the moment, I crack my neck and put up my guard. I'm aiming straight for that ugly mustache. And if that doesn't work, I'll cave in his skinny chest.

He calls across to me, "Okay, boy, let's have some fun."

I feel like destroying something. I forge forward, ready to knock his head off.

Bam!

Stars. Blackness. Fire.

Down and rolling.

The kick came from nowhere. Unbelievable that this bottom-heavy schlub was even able to get his foot off the ground.

He backs off—I'm known for attacking the legs from the ground.

I roll to my feet, crouched and swinging wildly. He stands back, chin tucked, and fists floating.

He's got the stance of a kickboxer.

How did I not see?

Overconfidence is weakness.

Careful.

Pinpoint.

The punches come like heat-seeking missiles. No flailing or wildness here.

Pop! I catch one in the forehead.

Shht! I skin my knuckles on his stubble.

"Close there, fella!"

You can hear the wet-meat smack of the hits all over the compound. Disgusting. Like a pissed-off butcher having a tantrum in the stockroom.

He's wary, but not afraid. Afraid of nothing.

Just like me.

We trade blows like fencers, parry and thrust. Graceful at first. You can feel the electric crackling in the air, the surging force between us. It's a chess game with blood.

His nose is bleeding. Gobs stick to his mustache.

My ear is split and throbbing. Sounds like a freight train.

Shuffle up a cloud of rusty dust.

Circling.

Vultures waiting for the guard to drop.

Darting in. *Whack!* Darting out.

The average street fight lasts just seconds. At ten minutes, we're still going, trading blows like titans with iron faces. At least he's stopped kicking.

Lips swollen. Cheeks numb. Breath flagging.

Behind each punch, it's all about letting go of that anger and fury, siccing the energy like a junkyard dog to tear and ravage, and then yanking it right back to fuel the next blow.

He grabs my arms, pulling me into a clinch.

"Quit?" he pants, flecking blood on my good ear.

"I will never quit," I snarl.

"Then we die here."

"Then we die."

I push him away and catch him square on the chin with a right.

Popcorn.

He shakes it off. Body shot to my ribs.

Gasping.

Drowning.

Leaning on each other trying hooks, uppercuts, knees.

Fluid seeps out of every orifice. Trying to escape the punishment.

I swing toward him and he clinches again.

"I think I gotta go to the hospital," he groans. "How 'bout a draw?"

"That's fine." Sweet relief.

We shake hands gingerly, broken bones grinding, trying not to wince.

A suit comes up. "What's going on, gentlemen?"

We both turn and glare, lips pulling back from blood-lined teeth in snarls he'll see in nightmares. He retreats, hands up disarmingly. "All right, all right, the fight's over. Say one of you tapped out. Whatever you do with the cash—I don't care." He must not be strapped, or else he'd act more confident.

The winnings plop on the table in thick parchment envelopes. Officially one of us wins, one of us loses; but neither of us cares which is which. We split the purses, six grand apiece, and hobble away from the ring.

"What's your name?"

"Paulie Gaeta. What's yours?"

"I'm Tex."

ooooo

Gaping into the phone, watching the counselor riffle through papers.

"*Tex* wants to take him camping?"

It makes no sense. Tex loves cocaine, and women with fake eyelashes and no rules. He loves gambling and cufflinks and crystal champagne glasses. He loves glitter and glamour and room service.

Hard to picture Tex in a tent.

"Yeah, Paulie, that's what he said. He wants to take Dante up to Vermont."

"What do you think about this?"

"Well, he loves the boy. He's been by several times in the last few years, *you* know."

What do you do when you're stuck in the pen and your best friend wants to take your son camping? Maybe you suspect he's trying to score the wife. Maybe you try not to think about it. Just sigh and frown into the phone.

"Yeah, that's fine."

"*You* tell him."

Smile when you tell your six-year-old boy, Go ahead and enjoy yourself. Tell old Tex hello.

Smile because a kid can hear your expression clear as words. Kids see a lot. Even when they see you never.

In the pictures, Tex the peckerwood has jheri curls and a diamond twinkle in his eye. He still has that stupid mustache, and even while keeping up a hard-ass attitude, how can you help missing the guy? At least he's looking out for Dante.

Being a daddy figure.

Jesus.

On the Inside, you get only a few minutes on the phone. Funny, for a guy who always absolutely loathed talking on the phone to dread that moment—

"Gaeta! Time's up. Hang up."

—when it's time to say goodbye.

ooooo

After the stalemate fight, Tex and I skipped the party and caught a helicopter ride to the nearest hospital. We both would have liked to stay, but even paid whores won't stick around long to chat when there's blood dripping from both ears and pus gumming together an eyelid or two.

It's all pretty hazy, like a red mist sort of blocks out the memory, but I remember stumbling through sterile hallways looking for someone to help us, lurching past bald kids in wheelchairs, past It's A Girl balloons, past stacks and stacks of flowers, past folks in scrubs checking their watches while gobbling down cafeteria food.

"Whoa," cried a nurse receptionist, leaping out of her chair with a pen-dangling clipboard. "What happened to y'all?"

"Construction accident," nodded Tex.

"Motorcycle crash," I shrugged.

She cocked an eyebrow and bent down to page somebody.

Tex leaned over, darted his good eye back and forth, and stage-whispered, "Where do I get my spongebath?" The nurse rolled her eyes and tugged on her ponytail.

"Over there." She jerked her head toward the Geriatric Wing.

Tex looked, and seemed to consider. "Can I just have one in my room? From you?"

"Sorry, I'm not into blood and black eyes. I'm a nurse." She wrinkled her nose and looked down at the clipboard. "Name?"

"Randall Tex Cobb."

Randall Cobb. It sounded so familiar I had to ask. "Randall Cobb? Where do I know you from?"

"Kickboxing? I'm undefeated."

"Please. I don't follow that shit. Something else?"

"You hear of Pedro Vega?"

No.

"You won't. I knocked him out in my first pro bout five years ago. I think he's still out."

"You're a pro boxer? What the fuck are you doing out in this circuit? You should be sweating in the lights, getting mad endorsement deals—not crouching in the shadow of a backhoe. C'mon!"

"I have a gambling problem."

"Gentlemen. If I *might* interrupt." The nurse handed us a pair of clipboards. "Fill out these forms, please. We'll be with you shortly. Meantime, here's some ice."

"Here, take my ice, Paulie. I think you took a worse beating back there."

"Fuck you."

So much for a throwaway. Tex was the top contender against Larry Holmes in the upcoming heavyweight title fight at the end of next year. Real glamorous legit boxing. And the man had a chin! Trust me. It was like punching a chunk of granite. If he could get inside Larry Holmes' reach, he'd win the belt for sure.

"So a gambling problem, huh?" I frowned as I filled out the clipboard paperwork with a sore hand. "What, like you can't gamble on pro fights, so you come out here for a little rough and tumble?"

"No, like I lost a bet to this asshole whose wager was he wanted to see me go at it without the gloves. To see if I—he says—could actually take a punch. You kiddin' me? I'm about to take on the Heavyweight Champion of the World. Seriously, Paulie, your little no-surrender game could've ruined my career instead of just my face."

"Wasn't much left to ruin."

"Ha funny. But that asshole never showed up after he set up this fight. And by then, I couldn't back down. Mob and all..."

"Some people."

"Mr. Gaeta? Mr. Cobb? Right this way please."

We limped after the nurse's bouncing ponytail into a room with two beds where we were told to sit and wait for the orderly who'd be in shortly to take us into X-ray.

ooooo

The day after the phone call with Dante, a C.O. interrupts a good game of chess. "Gaeta, Dr. Schwartz's office. Phone call." Fondling the knob of his nightstick, he cracks a wry grin. "Lucky sumbitch," he drawls, "Someone must like you."

This doesn't happen. It's a rare event when somebody from Outside is allowed to make unscheduled contact. Their rules keep everything orderly. To deviate is to invite creativity, imagination, memories of freedom.

"Hello?"

"Hi." Wife. Pissed.

The counselor—a great person to have as a friend—who let the call come through turns slightly away from the speakerphone in embarrassment, but listens anyway. Just doing his job.

"Sweetheart. How are you?"

"Would you like the phone number where your son is?"

The phone number? The hell? A questioning look at the counselor, who half-shrugs and slides a pad and pencil over.

She chirps the number and hangs up.

"Goodbye?" The receiver rattles into its cradle. "Can I make the call, Dr. Schwartz?" Even through a put-on smile, asking permission leaves a bitter aftertaste. Schwartz nods. His office is one of the few places in the joint where non-collect calls can be made.

Brrrrrr. The sound of a phone ringing somewhere. *Brrrrrr*. A grinding anticipation. *Brrr—*

"Caesar's Palace, Las Vegas, this is Rob, how may I be of service?"

There are many ways of keeping calm. All of them take immeasurable practice.

You can count one, two, three, four, five, six, seven, eight, nine, ten.

You can breathe deeply:

In.

Out.

You can screw your eyes shut and imagine a happy place.

You can bite your lip.

Gnaw your knuckles.

Do pushups.

The key is to channel your racing brainwaves toward something else.

"I'm sorry," grated carefully through clenched teeth, "I might've dialed the wrong number..."

He confirms that is not the case.

"Is there a Randall Tex Cobb there?"

"Oh yes sir," he croons, suddenly animated. "I believe he checked in yesterday morning. With his adorable son."

He's a dead man. Dead! When you're a thug, you know people who can make things happen. You can make sure Tex doesn't leave Caesar's Palace on his own feet. You can make sure his blood is splattered across the entire bank of penny slots. You can make sure he rolls snake eyes one last time.

The calming techniques work.

"Can I speak with him please?"

Practice makes perfect.

"Umm, yes. Give me one second. Who's calling please?"

"Just put him on."

The wait is interminable, amplified by the Muzak oozing from the phone. Who has the best connections to Vegas? Who could send someone there the quickest? Would Schwartz allow one more call?

"Hello?"

"Tex, you mother fucker."

"Paulie? Good to hear from you, buddy! You seem upset."

"My *son* is supposed to be in a *tent* in *Vermont*."

"Well we're playing blackjack at the moment."

"I've got a counselor right here, otherwise I'd tell you I'm gonna have you killed."

"Relax, pal. Talk to your boy before you kill me."

"Hello?"

"Dante?"

"Hi Dad!"

"What are you doing, Dante?"

"I'm playing blackjacks. I'm learning adding and minus-ing. And I'm learning remembering what cards I saw. Oh!...I wasn't 'posed to tell that."

"That's okay, buddy. What else have you been doing?"

"Yesterday we flew a helicopter! And then saw a show. I want to play music and sing."

"You do? What do you want to play?"

"Well I can sing the Natural Ant-hymn, listen!" He croons lustily, high voice crackling static against the phone receiver. "José, can you siiiing! By the dog's early light—!" Loud random rustling tapping scraping sounds as he drops the phone...

"Still there?" Tex back on the line. "This kid's great. The *balls* on him! I mean, if I could talk to women like he does..."

"Jesus, Tex, are you corrupting my boy?"

"Just teaching him how to play to stay on top of the world. His old man would be proud."

"I gotta hand it to you, buddy. You're an asshole, but it's a hell of a thing you're doing here. Put him back on for a minute."

"I got your back. I always do." He sniffles dramatically, probably swiping at an imaginary tear. "Hey, by the way, did you hear someone stole a *tank* in San Diego and drove around destroying half the city before they caught him and shot him?"

He continues a mostly one-sided conversation, telling jokes and stories until Schwartz gets impatient and cuts the call short.

ooooo

In prison they own your life. You're not your name, you're not your family's name, you're not your age, not your color, not your lineage, not your hometown.

You're 30583-012.

Your daily life depends entirely upon the largesse of the prison staff. Corrections Officers. Though if they're being honest, they really should call them Punitive Officers. The playing field is tilted in their favor, and if you fuck up and they catch you—and they always catch you—you're going to lose out. You're a pawn in a field of queens—an analogy that would be lost on most of the C.O.s, who'd think you're calling them queer. They're a reactionary bunch.

The primary difference between cons and screws, besides the color of the uniform and the hourly wage, is a divine directive of control. Underneath, everyone's just people.

Losing privileges like the weekly trip to the commissary is bad enough. Having visits cancelled, phone calls revoked, mail call held—these are things you come to rely on, and when they take them away, you feel like shit and there's nothing to break up the press of time. But for things like fighting, talking back, stealing, getting caught with drugs—the punishment is orders of magnitude worse.

The hole.

You can't imagine what it's like if you've never been. Panic sets in. Closed spaces with no escape. Sweaty palms, trembling, chills. The walls close in. The food slot grins like a jack-o'-lantern, always mocking.

Solitary is one of the worst punishments you can get. Officially, anyway. Sometimes a convict who really gets on the wrong side of the corrections staff will find himself with a price on his head. And then it's open season. There's no surviving that kind of sentence.

But mostly when you break the serious rules you wind up in the SHU for a little while—just until you cool off, pal. No contact with the other prisoners. No contact with the outside world. No fresh air. Limited interaction even with the screws who come by to fulfill mealtime duties.

It's just you. All of you. Every one of you.

All alone.

The food's the same—just less fresh. The mattress is hard. The molded bed is even harder, the fluorescent lights colder. Barred doors replaced by stamped steel and rivets.

The funny thing about solitary is that it's also known as protective custody. There's layers of meaning there. They put people in PC who'd get mauled in the blocks. People like pedophiles, celebrities, snitches, cops. For them it's a thing of survival. Amid the general population, those types wouldn't last long enough to be called "fish."

The Special Housing Unit is also where they store the craziest of the crazy killers, the guys who eat their victims or murder randomly. They isolate them to protect the gen-pop.

For everyone else, the hole is a reminder of why it's best to behave.

At first it's a relief to get away from people for a little bit. There's so much goddamn politics and games in prison, it's exhausting. But after the first few minutes, when you count on your fingers and toes, and lose track of how many more hours you'll be alone with barely more than a wingspan from wall to wall, awash in the sterile light of purgatory; hearing, seeing, smelling, feeling nothing but yourself, your yammering mind—it starts to eat away at you, and you lose track of the silence, broken only by the thud of your heart, the sound of your thoughts, the rasp of breath, the drumming of fingers, the grinding of teeth, the crawling of skin, the periodic clatter of food trays; as you listen to your hair growing, scratch a thousand times across the same patch of beard, calculate how many cubic centimeters of air are in this sixty-four square-foot room, wiggle your ears until they hurt, brush each tooth for a fifty-count if you're lucky enough to have a toothbrush—and still not pass more than a few minutes of what turns out to be the longest thirty seconds of your life, repeated ad infinitum, a series of moments with no beginning and no end, all strung together, all so badly the same in their emptiness that you have to fill them in somehow; maybe counting to sixty sixty times; once...twice...three times...four...five...six...seven...eight times...nine...ten...eleven...twelve...thirteen...fourteen... fifteen...sixteen...seventeen...eighteen...nineteen...twen-ty...twenty-one...twenty-two...twenty-three times, and then you're just counting, counting sheep, counting blessings, counting coup noticing how odd it is that the words for numbers have no quantitative consistency in structure or sound—like something you'd read but not understood in the *Theory of Relativity* about patterns and relationships of things and nothings—or maybe having the same dreaming moment over and over and over and over until the edges of everything blend together; or maybe puzzling through chess problems, writing letters to long-dead friends, fantasizing about burying your face in some tail, doing pushups and sit-ups and just pacing back and forth two and a half steps at a time until...hell, just *doing* it, just doing something, anything, everything to escape the nothing, and always questioning, always wondering, never ever ever quiet, as you sit there in silence saying nothing, voice cracked like old leather and impossible to regulate with no volume difference between thinking and screaming; thumbs aching from twiddling, toes tired from tapping; bored of breathing, bored of pacing, bored of thinking, bored of listening, bored of counting things, bored of being bored, trying not to think about the walls closing in, leaning in, reaching in; counting cinderblocks and wondering how often in life does a person ever spend more than a couple hours alone with thoughts, alone with himself; and there are moments of self discovery and inner peace and even something you might call *enlightenment*—according to the Dalai Lama—the awareness of being aware, the consciousness of consciousness, the soul soul-gazing outward, recognizing the body for what it is, and thoughts for what they are, and Being the entity behind the body and underneath the thought, and discovering that the inner voice is not You, but just an internal facade and a cloak of habits worn to protect your true self from drowning in the sensory saturation of the universe—a realization that is terrifying until it's uplifting, mystifying until it's clear, impossible until it's recognized; and Einstein's ghost joins up with Jesus to explain that there *is* no white-bearded, robe-wearing, staff-holding Man in the Clouds, no sandaled ego-sculptor with a mysterious name and omnipotent wrath, no celestial control tower directing things; that there is only what comes out of and goes into the space between your two eyes; that almost everyone has missed the point, that religion and philosophy and science are three of the many words for the same thing, and it turns out this is heaven and hell in the same room, all contained in uncountable electrical pathways burning their way through some gray matter, a transaction conducted through a few gallons of the same stale air, and energy *is* matter and matter *is* energy, and while you breathe it in and breathe it out and breathe it in and breathe it out, you become the room and the room becomes you, until the circulation is visible like fingerprint whorls, and the spirals of the airwaves start to dance before your eyes, and the whole cyclical nature of the universe becomes visible tangible audible smellable tastable knowable, and you sink into it, riding the waves of awareness, not so much floating *above* your body, but flowing into it so completely it disappears, joining in with something bigger—or not bigger, but a reality so microscopic it's only theoretical, taking away the limiting factors of time and space, breaking down the basic into the elemental, the elemental into the essential, and loving the Being loving the membership loving the absence of form, loving where, when, and how it takes you—until you snap awake—or rather drift off again—and your brain renews its filters for your sensory analysis, and you see only white-washed cinderblock, poured and painted concrete, a rolled-up mattress used for biceps curls, a splash of some food dropped decades ago; hear only the echoes of footsteps; smell only the heavy air and a perfume from long ago; feel only whatever you're touching and the wounds of the past; taste only tongue and teeth like steaks and croutons, and this continues on and on, back and forth, forever and ever because there are no clocks down here, not even the count, count, count, count that serves as the slow pendulum of time upstairs, and just when you think you're going to lose it again, this new idea that you've had before occurs, and the whole damn trip repeats itself—and you've exhausted only five minutes wallowing in the sentence.

You're stuck in a picture.

Stuck in the present of the moment, a being created from fragments of memory. Twenty-three hours worth of eternity, reliving each piece of a lifetime; thinking in strings of thought, helplessly conjuring the ghosts of the past. Then escorted down the hall in silence for a solitary shower. Which is the only thing that goes by fast.

And then more eternity. When you crunch it out like that, even a few days turns out to be a long time.

It's possible to get years.

ooooo

Ages ago, when I was thirteen and working as a janitor near the Fenway, I spent most of my spare time thrashing older kids in the lot behind the Southie projects where we played King of the Hill.

One of them, dusting himself off after a hard hiptoss that left him struggling for breath, shambled back up the hill with his hands up disarmingly.

"I'm done, I'm done, kid," he huffed. "I just wanna talk, okay?"

I didn't believe him for a second. He was a slick wop, maybe two or three years my senior, with a fat gold chain dangling over his wisps of chest hair that I'd almost ripped off mid-game. Even as an Italian—or maybe especially so—I never trusted guys like that.

"I'm Alonzo Battaglia," he said, offering a hand. I looked at it, sure that if I took it, he'd yank me down the hill. His friends had left, pissed off but beaten.

"Alonzo." I nodded once.

He stuffed his hand in his pocket. "I know you, Gaeta," he said. "Everybody knows you. You're a fucking asshole."

"Yeah, alright."

We stood at the edge of a splash of streetlight, sizing each other up. At our feet were a few bricks, some bottles, a waterlogged mattress. The hill was mostly a junk heap surrounded by a sagging fence. Prized only because of the value we all assigned that sacred spot on top.

"You interested in a job? A little pocket money?"

"I have a job."

"This one pays your full paycheck in one *day*, buddy. How 'bout that?"

"What I hafta do?"

"Run a sack for a bookie. Basically take a knapsack from one place to another."

"Why me?"

He scoffed and shook his head.

"Cuz you're tough as nails but no one would expect you to be a package boy. Cuz you're not con*nect*ed, buddy. You don't *know* anyone. Dig?"

I dug.

He knew me because when I got restless I ditched school during recess and humped my way to places like Cambridge and Brookline to romp with the kids who thought they were tough guys over there. Needless to say, they crumpled in the face of a Southie Italian.

What was the point otherwise? Grandpa was about to die of the same heart attack he'd been having for the last five years, and my parents weren't around much. The neighborhood was going to shit—the whole city was going to shit. School bored me to death. A social worker had recently started knocking around. There wasn't anyone I respected to stop me, and there wasn't any good reason not to get involved. This opportunity could finally let me get off the merry-go-round.

"Where?"

"That's the *spirit!*" he chuckled, pounding me on the shoulder. "Come on. We'll get you hooked up."

"When?"

"Right now. Man, you're wicked stupid, aren't you?"

I said nothing.

"Knows when to keep his mouth shut at least. That's an admirable trait."

He kept talking. Talking about rolls of money, talking about women waving diamonds, talking about filets and reefers and cases of wine that fell off trucks owned by guys he knew. Talking and talking and talking, as I walked alongside with my fists shoved in my pockets.

We finally wound up on Hanover in the North End, skirting broken cobblestones miles away from the projects where I lived. Feeling uncomfortable and suspicious, I walked a step behind Alonzo, watching him out of the corner of my eye as we strolled past shops and restaurants. Everything was Italian, but it was essentially uncharted territory, since I hadn't bothered to venture this close to the water, and I expected a fight at every corner.

Then he stopped.

I nearly bumped into him, entranced as I had become by the myriad restaurants. I'd never seen so many checkered tablecloths, or smelled so much rich food cooking. South Boston, I was beginning to realize, really sucked.

Alonzo turned around.

"You wait here, alright?"

"Yeah, sure. Whatever."

"Seriously," he hissed, grabbing my shoulder. "Don't move."

"The fuck?" I jerked my shoulder free. "What's wrong with you?"

"You wanna get shot before you even see the Boss?"

He explained that there were armed bodyguards in the vestibule who wouldn't hesitate to fill me with lead if they thought I was snooping around.

"But won't they think I'm trying to peek inside if I'm just standing here like an asshole?"

Alonzo rolled his eyes and sighed impatiently.

"Just wait here, okay?"

"Fine."

I stood there like an asshole, watching the flagpoles across the street fluttering American and Italian flags in the late-summer breeze. I suddenly realized how hungry I was, and that I hadn't eaten since chomping some toast before heading out to romp.

Then a girl walked by, tugging at her silky black hair and adjusting the strap of a knee-length purple dress that clung to the triangle between her upper thighs like a royal invitation to heaven. I watched her glide down the street with a book under her arm, until a hand closed around my neck and a voice rasped in my ear:

"Hey, *carogna*, you lookin' at my sister or *what*? Let's do some business."

Alonzo.

Jesus. I wanted to cave his face in. His very words seemed to profane the angelic vision of the smooth-faced girl walking under a halo of trimmed bangs. I couldn't believe this slimy JD was related to her.

"That's your sister? Christ, man, you must have a bitch of a time keeping your hands offa her when she's sleeping."

He stopped. Took a step forward and looked me straight in the eye.

"You listen to me, ciucciacazzi," he growled. "You don't mess with my sister. Ever. You hear? I could stab your ass to death, and nothing would happen to me because my dad's a lawyer."

"Yeah, yeah, I'm just playin' around," I lied, hands open disarmingly. I had every intention in the world of getting past that lavender dress and into the secret garden beneath. Just a matter of time, I figured. She was perfect. Plus someone just told me I couldn't.

"Yah, yah. Come with me, ya jerk. And holy shit, you gotta hear this: A bunch of kids just took over Harvard. It's all over the news. The cops are laying it on."

What the hell was going on in the world? Seemed like everything was crumbling beneath our feet.

ooooo

Sometimes it's better *not* to know your opponent. I could do, for example, without the knowledge that this Tongan has killed the last five guys he fought.

Tongans, if you've never had the dubious pleasure of meeting one, are basically like Samoans: big and mean. This one is bad enough to look at; three -hundred-fifty grim pounds of meat, hair like an explosion. Big hands, big ass, big calves, big waist. When I see him, for the first time in my life I want to skip a fight. I'll take the two grand. Get me outta Dodge.

"Hey," I say to one of the masters of ceremony, "I don't need this fight. Give me a ride out of here."

He looks at me with a sort of sneer. "*That's* your ride, pal," he offers, jerking his thumb toward the Caterpillar excavator.

Point taken.

The spectators start to arrive, stepping out of the back seats of Bentleys, Rolls Royces, Maybachs, and the occasional helicopter. Ten gamblers per fight, plus minions, bodyguards, and money handlers. The corporate guys who run the show meet each one personally, and accept their cases full of money with friendly smiles. A million dollars cash. Which is chump change to people like these.

Some go right for the food, digging through crab legs, prime rib, lobster claws, pawing at shrimp the size of my fist, quaffing fine wine by the gobletful. Others peruse the group of escorts brought in by the corporation. I'll tell you something: the hookers hanging around Miami and Texas and Southern California are the finest. All the more reason to win this fight.

I do my best to ignore what happens next.

What happens next is a show on a raised platform near the cloth-covered dining tables where a guy with a dick to his knees—I mean, this guy *trips* over his cock—starts fucking some stoned girl while she licks a donkey's balls.

I shit you not.

This is the kind of sick twisted entertainment these people go ape over.

They laugh and cheer.

So this freak is up there humping away, *slish slish slish* while guys in six-thousand-dollar suits are doubled over, choking on their cigars, and this poor girl grins a dopey grin. Even loaded with tranqs or China White, I still don't understand how she's not shrieking in pain.

Slap slap slap slap, and he's grunting like a chimp, practically hooting for emphasis.

Point of fact, I feel bad for the donkey. He'd probably rather be out munching fresh grass.

Already changed into dungarees and an old sweatshirt, I turn away and draw stick figures in the dirt until it's over.

When it's done, a suit gets up on the same stage, adjusts his tie, and pulls out some poster-sized photographs and snippets of newspapers and legislation. He explains current DEA procedures, enumerates the latest legal information including important cases, and lectures on federal involvement—keeping all these felons up to speed.

I listen up when he talks about cocaine, and from everything he says, it seems my investment will pay dividends.

"Disco," he shrugs. "Nose candy. The kids love it."

A couple other guys come up, present their credentials, and list off various new methods of cloaking money, warn against modes of trafficking that have been discovered, and hand out printouts. These are some very astute people, too, people who probably would be working for the other side if the pay weren't such a joke. Anyone ever tells you crime don't pay, go ahead and steal his wallet when he's not looking. Teach him something about the world. You'll be doing him a favor.

They always remind us, before arriving for a fight, not to tell anyone where we're going, because we might not be coming back. Chilling. Interesting the impact that has on how you live your life.

I cinch up my boots and peel off my shirt. A tub of Vaseline sits on my knee. Somewhere to my left, some heavy rounds rip through the air, perforating a Jeep with frightening ease. No wonder the IRA is having a fucking field day, terrorizing folks into quivering submission.

A rocket-propelled grenade snakes toward the vehicle.

In front of me, two kids are getting ready to step into the ring—really just a circle of tramped-down dirt—for the first fight. I've been there. Your first few fights are exhibition for a grand or two, until you're deemed worthy. That's when you go sign a contract for a hundred fights.

That's when they have you by the balls.

Doesn't seem like too many when you're first hearing about it, especially thinking about the million cash grand total, but get to your 80th fight or so and—win or lose—you got knuckles like golf balls, aching muscles, split skin, and the same black eyes for years. Nothing to do but grit your teeth and find that evil gem of focus buried beneath all the bruised meat.

Fill the coffers. Get the adrenaline fix. Soothe the ego.

There's something about being a fighter. Something superhuman. I don't mean I'm tucking myself into spandex and flying around saving people.

Something deeper.

Like I'm more connected to myself. Aware of every part of my body and its relation in space. I can feel every muscle twitching as I jump some jacks to warm up. I hear the blood pumping into my fists as I grunt out some pushups. Skin tingles in the breeze like a million little motion sensors. Heels lift from the ground. Twinkle-toes; warrior mode.

In this exhibition round, Kid One is pummeling Kid Two. Kid Two is a black kid with a Boston area code tattooed on his shoulder, and despite how I feel about hood-rat types like him, we're more or less geographical associates, and I want him to win. However, he's blowing it, and if he gets maimed, it's his own damn fault for not hitting harder, being better, fighting fiercer.

There's no excuses. Not fucking *ever*.

I'm trying desperately not to think of the Tongan. I have no doubt I can take him, but in this one, I slip up once—I don't get a second chance. I focus, or I wind up dead.

A guy getting dropped into a pre-dug hole is all arms and legs and floppy head. Like a Cabbage Patch doll. Muscle tone gone. Pants freshly stained. If I think about that, I'm done for.

There's only one thing I need to think about to have a good fight. If I keep that image in mind, I win.

I step into the circle. Concentrating, picturing, remembering. I see this giant in place of Mikey Stone, squatting and unloading on my chest.

Bets fly, both aboveboard through the corporation's bookie, and by semi-sanctioned murmurs and nods. One of the favorite bets is half a mil on whether someone will get killed. People always root for death, even in something legit like the Indy 500.

We, who are about to die, salute you.

Crowd fades.

Eyes narrow and focus.

Fists clench.

A pulse thrumps against my jaw.

I see only one thing. This juggernaut rushing at me screaming bloody murder, wild hair bouncing like a demonic counterweight.

If he hits me before the ref says *go*, I win.

If he hits me with my guard down, I die.

RRROOOAAAGGGGHHHHH bellowing charging like a bull.

I stand.

"Shh," I say, with a finger to my lips. "The fuck's wrong with you?"

He stops in his tracks, retreats to his side—I swear—with a curl of smoke rising from a nostril.

Hands up now, on guard. Active defense. Ready to fight.

But the truth is, I'm holding them up to see if they're shaking.

Steady like a surgeon.

The ref shakes his head at the Tongan and double-checks with the bosses before murmuring, "Alright, gentlemen—go."

This ain't the WBA. There's no handshake or bell. There's no *Let's Get Ready to Rummmble!* Everybody knows the rules. Everybody knows the stakes.

RRRROOOAAAGGGGHHHHH and he's charging again, forehead down, balled hands up. A cymbal-crashing monkey.

He pounds across and cocks a fist.

At the last second, I slip inside his left, and twist an uppercut as he swings past. The impact vibrates down my arm, rippling across my chest and into my right side.

The Tongan drops like he's been shot.

Badda-*bing*. That's how you *do* a motherfucker.

I stand ready, daring him to get up. His lips blow a pink bubble which picks up dust and pops. Then another. He groans faintly.

Thumping adrenaline boils through my veins, teeth bared in a snarl twitching toward a smile. Eyes flashing wild.

He's out.

Resisting the urge to pound my chest, I stalk off like David, ready to have my pick of Goliath's treasure and women. The fight hadn't even lasted long enough for me to sweat through the Vaseline.

Some escorts sitting around a poker table wave me over as I pass. "Hey, you just won, right?"

"Yeah," I grin and wince at the blonde who spoke. "Can you fix a broken hand?"

She frowns. "Um..."

"Then I'll talk to you later." I pinch her chin and wink, turning and heading to the shower, knees sort of trembling in the aftermath.

ooooo

Once he'd gotten the Don's permission to introduce me, Alonzo led the way into a glass storefront. The sign overhead read, *Brothers' Suppliers*. A pair of vacuum cleaners sat in the display window, framing a lime-green recliner chair.

I looked left and right as I walked in, but saw no goons. Still distracted by the beauty that had passed me in the street, I automatically followed Alonzo into the back of the store through a connection into a restaurant next door.

Garlic.

The sharp heady smell of sautéing herbs nearly knocked me over as we passed from the jumbled storage-closet warehouse into the commercial kitchen. A fat guy in a white frock tilted his head inquisitively, before recognizing Alonzo with an upward nod, and beckoning us into a back room off the main floor.

"Alonzo. Benvenuto," called a disembodied voice.

"Padrino. This is Paulie. He's ready to work, like I told you."

"Send him over," urged the velvety voice purring from a corner booth. "Hungry, kid?"

I nodded.

He shoved a plate full of cheese and olives and salami toward me, and splashed a bread plate with the olive oil jar from the middle of the table. He wore a white carnation tucked into the lapel of his violet suit, and a wide tie that was out of fashion, but looked new.

"So Alonzo tells me you're interested in a job. That you aren't to be fucked with."

"So they say," I murmured, eyeing the plate.

"Eat."

I obeyed.

"Alonzo told you how much this pays." It wasn't a question. More of an affirmation.

I nodded.

"You get a hundred-fifty bucks," he continued. "You get fifty when you pick up the bag, and another hundred after."

"Yeah," I nodded. "I'll do it."

"Of course you will." The Don explains that someone will be ready with the bag in front of his restaurant at nine the next night. All I had to do was take the bag, hump it around a few blocks, and end up in the club where his client would be waiting with a ledger. I had to make the exchange and bring the paper back. Upon my return I'd be treated to a full-course meal. Plus the money. And most importantly an escape from the slow-roasting death of my pre-scripted life.

ooooo

After I delivered the bookie's package and brought the information back to the Don, he beckoned me closer.

"Want to double that, kiddo?"

Uh, yeah. Of course. What kinda dumb question...?

I nodded politely.

"I know a guy needs a hundred-dollar loan. You give it; you collect on it; you make another fifty bucks interest on toppa that. Then you finish *that* job, I got another job for ya—for another fifty. *Capice*? Double-down."

The hard way.

"Yeah. Sure. Whatever."

He showed me the address and told me don't let the guy fuck around—do what I gotta do. "Don't be afraid to drop my name," he said.

He told me give the guy two weeks to pay back and take no compromises. He'll snivel and beg, but give him two weeks. His grandmama dying—two weeks. His kid in jail—two weeks. No backing down in this line of work.

Then the Don picked a thread from his buttonhole and turned back to his plate as if we'd already left the restaurant.

Alonzo tagged along, leaning in to whisper advice, backing me up with his little snubnose .22 popgun with its handle and trigger wrapped in athletic tape, a weapon I wanted, even though I'd never fired one before.

He talked a big talk about having done all this before, about how it's so easy, and how he almost hoped something *would* go wrong so he could *cap a mothafucka*. That's what he said, like some kind of jazzy pimp.

I fought a surge of disappointment rising in my throat like bile. The Don was quiet, calm, level-headed—almost square. I was expecting Tony Camonte. What I got was a velvet-tongued loan shark in a silk suit. He wasn't ordering me to kill Whitey Bulger or sending me to bribe senators or outlining a plan to con his way into the diamond game. He was using me to do his business laundry, to pick up his spare change, to run his low-grade errands. That's what you get, I suppose, for sneaking into Paul Muni flicks for your education.

The pavement was crumbled in spots, hunks of asphalt scattered like chunks in a litterbox. Bits of paper and Dunkin Donuts cups lurked in corners, and cast-off parking tickets whiffled in the breeze. Here and there a ragged Red Sox flag hung limp.

The door of this Jew Rosen's apartment building hung open, yawing like a drunk, and screeching faintly on uneven hinges. Three days' worth of newspapers leaned against the stoop. A large bowl with dried-stuck fragments of noodles teetered on the edge of a wicker chair. A blank sheet of note paper fluttered in the breeze.

"The fuck is this?" I glanced warily at Alonzo.

"Ugly." He shivered.

Knock knock—

The door creaked open just as my knuckles grazed the wood for another strike.

"Uh, 'lo?"

"Marty Rosen?"

"Yeah?"

"We heard...um...heard you could use some cash."

The claw wrapped around the door twitched, and the door swung open. The foyer was dimly lit, and so darkly painted you couldn't see a goddamn thing. A thin cigar smoldered in a cereal bowl. A cat—or something—flitted past.

"What are you guys, fifteen? You boys hungry?" We shook our heads. "Thirsty?"

"Goddamnit, no! This ain't a social fucking *visit*, buddy. You want to do business? Or go fuck yourself?"

Alonzo nodded behind me.

I was nervous that Alonzo was the one holding the gun. I felt like a worm wriggling on a hook. But I couldn't let that get in the way.

"Don Aberto said I should cut off your fingers if you fuck around with me."

The gaunt man at the door laughed nervously. Then he reached a hand out placatingly.

"Kid, just give it to me, okay? Just give it."

"When will you pay back?"

He seemed surprised I'd even asked, probably expecting due dates announced matter-of-factly, with no wiggle room. Hell—I was new at this.

"Well, I've got to make the buy, and then cut it up, and then bag it up, and then—"

"I don't need your fucking life story," I amended. "When?"

"Three weeks...?"

"You have thirteen days."

Then I turned and left.

Behind me Alonzo kissed the barrel of his gun, and pointed it at the junkie.

"See ya! Wouldn't wanna be ya!"

Outside, he punched my arm, laughing. "That was great! You're wicked pro, kid."

"Put the gun away. It's broad daylight, are you stoopid?"

We squinted in the sunlight.

"So now what?"

"Now you just wait a few days, and then go back to spook him a little. Anticipation is your baddest weapon."

Take advantage of that most human of fears—the unknown, or rather the imagined. Vague promises of pain, with a few tangible reminders here and there.

"What if he don't come through?"

"We'll worry about that when we get there, huh? Let's have a drink."

ooooo

The morning before a visit is the worst. You've spent the previous week hiding out, lurking in your cell reading, steering clear of any areas where a fight might break out, avoiding anything that might cause trouble. Anything that might justify loss of visiting privileges.

Can you imagine showing up at the castle, excited to see your loved one, sitting down as they call the names of inmates with visits scheduled? Can you imagine just sitting there, not hearing your name? You've come hours, planned for days, taken time off work, skipped school, caught the bus, hitched a ride, borrowed a car—just to sit there alone, until some conscientious guard finally tells you Sorry, your brother friend husband son boyfriend client father was caught with contraband and wasn't allowed a visit today.

You'd go home feeling miserable, feeling abandoned, feeling rejected. Wondering why you bothered coming in the first place, the ungrateful bastard. But you go home. Home.

The morning before a visit, it's wise to skip breakfast. Everyone's grumpy in the morning—some hungover, some constipated, some sleepless from nightmares—and there's no way to predict what wrong word will send someone over the edge and cause a brawl and the subsequent lockdown. Or even if nothing like that happens, you might get in trouble for taking too much coffee, or for sitting next to two guys doing a drug deal. You might get shoved in line, and have to defend yourself.

There's too many ways to get in trouble. It's worth the gnawing stomach to stay away.

And if you make it through the morning, the few hours before the visit are even harder. What if they don't show? What if they get cold feet? What if they get turned away at security? What about traffic? Illness? Speeding tickets? What if they decide not to come?

You stand there, stomach growling, feet restless, surrounded by a dozen other shifty nervous guys. Behind the locked door, visitors are finding tables, following directions, obeying staff. Tapping their fingers and waiting.

Then they let the inmates in one by one to find their people and make nice.

"You know I grew up thinking you worked overseas, and that's why we never saw you?"

Not so much accusatory as matter-of-fact, Dante launches the conversation with no hesitation, as if continuing an old chat. Shaking hands firmly like a man, he says Pops—because Paulie would be disrespectful and Dad would just be weird. Can't help but agree. Even though it hurts.

"Yeah." Times like these you avert your eyes and examine your fingernails. "I'm sorry, Dante."

"And then when I found out, Mom wouldn't let me come here or even call you."

"Yeah, that's when she had me stop calling, and write letters instead."

Visitors have to be at least sixteen years old to see an inmate without a parent present. You can argue till you're blue in the face that he *would* be with a parent, but as it turns out, sense of humor is not a prereq for federal employees. Dante got his driver's license six weeks ago.

"Bitch," he says.

"Hey, kiddo, don't talk about your mother that way. C'mon."

"Why not? You know it. I know it." His eyes twinkle as he adds, "Let's *agree* on something, Pops."

"Don't matter. You respect your parents. Even if they're a bitch and an old con."

"Respect parents, huh?" he asks. "I wonder how grandma and grandpa are doing?"

The kid's got a point. Little shit. "So how's school? Any girls I need to know about?"

He chuckles, glances at the tabletop to hide a blush, and drums his fingertips before looking up and shrugging.

"C'mon! I bet they're lining up for you. You remember how to play one against the other?"

"Eh, I dunno, Pops," he hedges. "I'm pretty into this one. She's in the choir."

"She like your singing?"

He nods.

"Talk to her?"

He shakes his head. "She's not like the girls Tex used to have me talk to when he took me places. She's different."

"What, not blonde? Smart? Actually pretty? Clean? Reasonable tits?" It's difficult to remember what sort of language is considered appropriate outside the walls. Dante visibly relaxes.

"I dunno. I just like her."

"Good. Like whoever the fuck you want to like. But ball up and talk to her, buddy! Ask her to give you notes on your solos. Take her to the opera. Shit, tell her you like her haircut or her new bag."

He shrugs again, nodding. "Yeah, I guess you're right."

"Always remember, women are just like you. Minus the package. And add some emotional baggage. And far *far* more pretty."

ooooo

This girl Holly Chen reminds me of Alonzo's sister. She's pretty as hell, with a soft wide mouth that laughs at everything. When she thinks I'm not looking, she tugs at her shimmery dress to keep the low-cut low. The fact that she's Chinese instead of Italian makes no difference. Similar pouty lips. Sultry dark eyes with a dab of bronze at each inside corner. A ready smile filled with crisp white teeth.

Alonzo would come after me with a baseball bat if he heard I compared his little sister to an LA hooker. He'd also come after me with a baseball bat if he knew I used to make it with his sister in the back of their pop's Towncar. Hell, there's a lot of reasons for Alonzo to come after me with a bat.

But that's another story. Alonzo's long dead. The survival rate of a street-level Mafioso is even worse than for a death-circuit bare-knuckle fighter. Especially if there's a war on. And there's always a war on in the streets. Only no one ever cares about it as long as civilians don't die, in part because the Feds are always involved in their own much more public wars.

I nod and smile, half-listening to Holly's story. I've had attention problems my whole life, which drove my parents and teachers nuts, and nearly got me in trouble with Don Aberto on a number of occasions. I have the hardest damn time focusing on anything for very long, especially the drone of someone talking. My mind just wanders.

Except when I'm fighting.

"I left Beijing again when I was almost sixteen," she says, tapping her steak-knife on the tablecloth.

I blink and refocus on this girl, Holly Chen, the one I approached after the fight, after my shower. Not the blonde girl who half stood, expectantly.

Sit down, I told the blonde. *Not you.*

I turned to the exotic-looking girl next to her, far prettier, but in a quieter way. *How long have they paid you for?* I asked, and sat down on the bench.

Four hours, she said, glancing at her watch. *Twenty minutes from now.*

Come with me. We're leaving. I bet you I can get you to give me a freebie.

No way, never. She sidled up and brushed an imaginary bit of lint from my shoulder. *You're cute,* she smiled and shook her head, *but never.*

Okay forget it. I'm starved—let's just go grab a bite to eat. Old fashioned-style, where I drop you off in a cab afterward. On me.

I clear my throat. "Beijing? Alone? No family?"

"Nope." She smiles proudly. "All on my own again."

"How's your porterhouse?" I ask, nodding at her plate.

"So good," she murmurs, closing her eyes.

I lift my wine glass and sip from it, staring at her over the rim. Her chest sparkles under the chandelier, subtle glitter of whatever lotion she put on pulling me in toward the soft hollow with each chance flash.

"I can't believe she sent you to timeout in Beijing."

"Yeah," she chirps indignantly, and glances at her lap. She flicks her hair back, slicing off another thin strip of tenderloin.

"Your mom just *sent* you there? Fuckin' pisser!"

Surprise! Welcome to Beijing. You stay: I'm leaving.

"Yeah. I couldn't behave in California."

Go to China. Learn Lesson.

"And you came back—all better, she thought?"

"Of course. Look at me now. I got hella cash." She leans back and smirks. "I'm a rich Chinese. The good life. And no thanks to her. I could pick up this tab, and it wouldn't be such a big thing. And all cash.

Economically independent, and tax-free. Reagan would be proud, right?"

I sit back and cross my arms. "Maybe I should just let you pick up the check, then."

And then, I swear, she bats her eyelashes at me. Like the movies. Gorgeous, sweeping eyelashes, with just the right amount of sparkle.

"You cannot imagine the things I would do to you," I say, spearing a square of filet on my knife and chomping it with a grin. She sits up ramrod straight, and pulls her shoulders back, smiling at the edge of her mouth.

"Hmm, I've heard that one before," she says coyly, cocking an eyebrow. "Like what, for example?" she adds, reapplying lip gloss.

"A magician never reveals his secrets. I wouldn't want you to get too excited."

"Tsh. Whatever," she says, looking at her steak quickly and carving off another piece.

I chew a bite.

Chew.

Chew.

You're supposed to chew a hundred times, right? To make sure you don't choke. That little bromide was pounded into me as a kid to keep me from talking at the table. It helps as a time delay too.

Then I soften the blow.

"Hush, no pouting." I reach across and tap her lips gently. "You said no freebies anyway. I don't pay for sex. So here we are: charming friends having a nice meal, eh?"

She smiles expectantly. I wink and take another bite of steak. Her shoulders settle as she laughs, resting a hand on the table comfortably while squeezing my knee with the other.

I'm in. Past the hard edges. Silvery edges worth polishing, to be sure—but edges nonetheless. I'm into the soft inner folds, neatly nuzzled against the pearl within.

Now I get to enjoy myself.

ooooo

"Enjoy yourself, Dante! Never be afraid of love, buddy." How to explain to a lovestruck sixteen-year-old boy that his angelic vision is no more than a living, breathing, dancing, eating, shitting, thinking human being with the usual interests and odors and fears? How to explain that he has no reason to fear his deified image? Tex hadn't known to teach him the difference between a sheath and a love.

The image of Dante, whether actual or imagined, is always accompanied by a wave of guilt and the press of history. To think just one neglected rubber and a sort of shotgun wedding bridge the gap between his existence and the world.

He talks about school, weaving stories in the air with his hands, and explains a new subway fee system the Boston MBTA is implementing. As he speaks, the clock watches over everybody, with skinny arms folded across its chest and a stern grimace on its face.

The buzz of conversation does nothing to drown the slurping noises of a few inmates kissing girlfriends or wives.

"I'm going to Disney World on spring break," he suddenly remembers. "With the orchestra."

The lieutenant calls out, interrupting a dozen conversations, letting everyone know, just five minutes left. So goddamn short, these visits—you have to cram years and months into a few minutes. Just when you're finally warmed up to the visitor and the conversation, it's time to part ways again for who knows how long.

Obviously Dante can't visit often. There's school and extracurriculars and his mother to contend with. There's his little girlfriend and homework and healthy sleep patterns. There's the idea that preventing him from coming to see the prison will keep him from taking up residence here someday.

"Here's my cell number, Pops. Mom doesn't look at my phone. Call me."

That slip of paper—torn from a piece of algebra homework—still holds its place of honor between the pages of a dog-eared and annotated *Iliad* on a tiny shelf mounted on the cinderblock cell wall, the digits written on it relegated to rote memory.

ooooo

Five days after visiting the junkie dealer's house on our first loan assignment, Alonzo and I were back, dribbling a soccerball up the street toward his broken stoop. On the sidewalk, I punted the ball *BOOM* against his door.

After a moment it creaked open.

"Hey! Sorry, mister." I crossed my arms and smirked with all the contempt a fourteen-year-old could muster. "Toss it back, wouldja?"

This guy Rosen stooped slowly to pick up the ball. And then he smiled.

What—?

"Glad you boys are here. I've got your money."

Already?

"Come in. I have it in an envelope inside."

I frowned and glanced at Alonzo, doubtful and stormy with suspicion. Smelling a trap. Alonzo shrugged. I adjusted the .22 in my waistband as we mounted the stairs, but decided to pull it out and hold onto it inside my sweatshirt pocket.

The hallway was dim and smelled sharp, as if someone had just rubbed every surface with bleach or ammonia. A table in the kitchen was strewn with scales and tablespoons, ripped plastic bags and twist-ties. There was a clicking fuzz like the end of a record coming from the other room. A faint film of pastel powder covered the surface of everything on the table. The rest of the room sparkled like Mr. Clean's balls.

My lip curled slightly, and I raised an eyebrow at Alonzo.

"Looks like you've been busy, old man."

"Hey, man." He looked indignant. "I'm twenty-seven."

"Yeah, like he said. Old man. Where's the money?"

He reached into a desk drawer and withdrew an envelope. I counted four crisp twenties and two tens.

"This is just—"

"The principal. Yeah. I figured we could negotiate the interest, since I'm paying early. I'm trying to pay my way back to New York."

My sneer twisted into a snarl.

"Hey, go fuck yourself, alright? I ain't the fucking Federal Reserve. You owe me one-fifty, buddy."

He raised his hands in mock surrender like a politician, worlds different from the paranoid and itchy fixxer we'd seen the other day, despite a sheen of sweat on his forehead.

"Suit yourself, then. I was going to see if you'd be interested in investing in my next deal instead. Oh well, no sweat."

I took the additional fifty he handed over, and turned on my heel.

"We'll think about it," Alonzo said over his shoulder before slamming the door.

On the porch, Alonzo grabbed my shoulder. "Hey, why don't you want in? That guy clearly has his shit in line."

I kicked the wicker chair, sending it clattering across the porch.

"Just 'cause he disinfects his whole vacant house when he's cutting That Boy don't mean he's got his shit together. He's still a fucking junkie who uses his own shit. Didn't you see the track marks?"

"That boy?" Alonzo looked puzzled.

"Yeah. Heroin. You never heard That Boy?"

"No way, man, that ain't a thing."

I was surprised. "Yeah, that's what the niggers call it. Cuz it makes you its bitch. And coke's That Girl, cuz you just keep putting your face in it and all you get in return is an empty wallet and a funky taste on your tongue."

Alonzo stared, and then broke into hysterics, slapping his leg and nearly falling off the porch. "Magnifico! Oh, it's *per*fect! Troppo, troppo. Paulie, man, I'm *so* glad you lived among the darkies."

"Alonzo, shut the fuck up. Let's get this cash back to the Don."

"And then we'll grab a drink." It was almost a question. I wasn't used to people deferring to me, especially older people, but the prospect both thrilled and filled me with contempt.

I rolled my eyes. The guy could barely drive, but when he discovered that he knew enough people to get him into bars and clubs around Boston, he'd gone apeshit for booze and loud music. He thought he was some kind of immortal, because he never had hangovers.

I eventually got sick of telling him he slept too late to get hangovers, and if he'd actually roll himself out of bed at a reasonable hour, he'd probably feel like dying.

You expect me to be up at the crack of noon? he'd joke, as if he'd made it up.

Go fuck yourself, you spoiled son-of-a-crooked-lawyer. I always smiled along with the shit he spewed, but I knew his role in my route was that of a guide. You lean on them until you *get* to El Dorado, and then they're left behind, acknowledged later with a polite nod.

"Yeah, we'll grab a drink." I threw my arm around his shoulder with a saccharine camaraderie. "But I have to get up early for work. Not all of us suck on silver bullets when we go nighty-night."

To my surprise he shrugged me off.

"Who are you kidding, Gaeta?" He nodded his chin at the little revolver stuffed in my shirt. "How long you think that day job is going to last? You gonna tell the Don 'No I can't do a job for ya 'cause I gotta go in to work in the morning'? Please. You're cosa nostra now. Like it or not, boy, you in like Flynn."

I regarded him. Then he broke into a smile. "And don't pretend you don't *love* it. The power!"

The power. The sense of belonging to something. The fearfulness in life draining away. And the money. I hated being a janitor. I loved the money I smelled with this new thing. Our thing. Cosa nostra.

A few days later at work in the Fenway, a pickup drove up and stopped, with a laborer aboard coming to fix something or meet someone.

Mikey Stone.

With no goons.

After I took care of the bastard, I stuffed my fists in my pockets, and pulled off my blood-spattered sweatshirt. Keeping my head down, I jogged casually toward the river. At Mass Ave, I crossed Storrow and crouched below the bridge, tossing the sweatshirt into the water. Shivering slightly, I headed east toward the North End.

A runner bounded past, and I ducked my head.

Idiot! Keep calm. Breathe slow. Get that heart rate down. Calm. I forced myself to breathe, and pulled my hands out of my pockets, relaxing fingers and wrists. I walked with a measured pace—but fast—as if I had somewhere important to be.

Somewhere important, like the safety of the North End, where I knew people who weren't afraid of police. Of getting caught. People who knew that getting uncaught was just a matter of greasing the right palms, or cracking the right heads—whichever came first.

A woman reeled in her dog as she passed me. A bicyclist whistled me out of the way. I walked in a daze, breathing hard, still thriving on the thrill of adrenaline, but feeling the imminent collapse after it used up my energy. If only I had change for a phonebooth, I could call Alonzo. I'd blown my quarters on a Coke in the morning. A gust of wind filled my nostrils with the rich sweetness of horse shit, and I gagged, sure that I would die at the hands of some madman.

I might've just killed a man.

Fuck that, hissed my own voice in my head. He was no man. He was a worm, and you just rid the world of that scum.

But what if he's dead? I just killed a guy. That's forever.

That coward was a piece of shit, I argued, and if he's dead, the world is now better off.

How true. But still.

I need to get out of here.

A Coast Guard interceptor curved across the Charles, heading for the harbor. I kept walking.

In the Esplanade I crossed the street toward the park, where a few college kids were flinging Frisbees, and a guy was tossing a stick for his dog. A handful of hippies were standing around. Two or three police officers strolled and chatted, faces relaxed and hands shoved in pockets or hooked on belts. From a bench a woman dangled long stems of grass into a stroller, cooing and burbling.

Disgusted, but not sure why, I walked faster. What had Grandpa said? The disdain of youth. Whatever. Philosophies of a crotchety old man lost meaning with the clammy fingers of what-have-I-just-done groping at me from every crack in the sidewalk. I had to get to the

North End. My new home base. Where I'd be protected by people who valued me.

I crossed behind the State House where a herd of angry people were yelling about something called "my lie." Whose lie? The golden dome overhead burned in the sunlight, and I crossed onto North Street where I bummed a cigarette from a Suffolk student on her way from class. Inhaling the calming smoke, I crossed the highway into the North End.

The smell of garlic washed over me, and I swear I nearly cried with happiness and relief. I loped down the cobblestones and burst into Don Aberto's restaurant. His court.

There was a cluster at the maître d' stand.

The restaurant buzzed with business, a strange hour for people in tuxedos to be standing around with martinis and wine glasses, gossiping and waiting to be seated. Servers bustled around busboys, and a pianist pounded away at a baby grand in the corner near the window. It was loud. Too loud.

"May I help you, Signore?" The maître d' bowed and scraped, carrying out his duties with an odd grace.

"I need to talk with Don Aberto. It's urgent," I added.

"Sir, I'm not sure who you're talking about...?"

"The owner, man. Aberto Bello. Where's your goddamn boss?"

He leaned close. "Sir, you smell like bleach and garbage. I'm not going to let you in here. Who are you?"

"Fucking—!" I lowered my voice and looked around. "Look, I work for him, alright? Can you just let him know one of his boys is here?"

He must have seen something of the fear and ruthless excitement in my face, because he narrowed his eyes. "What's your name?"

"I don't know if he knows my name. I just started working for him. Come on. Please just tell him."

He nodded and said, returning to his officious restaurant tone, "Just a moment, sir, and I'll be right back with you."

I didn't wait long. The din and drone of the restaurant got to me at the same time as I realized I had no real need to be so scared. No one knew that goon. He never did anything by the rules, and no one could connect him to me. He probably had dozens of fake names, and almost certainly never paid taxes or anything. There was nothing official, but even so—fuck!—I had no clue of the law.

Suddenly I wondered if he still had my sled.

The sidewalk was wet in places, a result of bars tossing slop buckets in preparation for the night's activities. I walked toward Alonzo's favorite bar, the one he'd be at every night of the week if his father didn't patronize it on Wednesdays and Fridays. On those nights, Alonzo drank bottles of beer on his roof with his older cousins, or chicks he knew, burning down cheap cigars and complaining about the rigorous lives of such as they.

Bullshit.

I don't know why I sought Alonzo, but I needed to tell somebody something. Sometimes truths will out, no matter how best-kept-secret they are. It's like money burning holes in pockets. It's just the nature of the goddamned beast. The reason most criminals get caught. The sacred little thing called Conscience.

At some point, I knew, I'd have to learn how to really bury that nagging voice. But tonight, I needed to spill the beans.

"Is Alonzo here?" I felt like a little boy, asking the doorman if there were Cool People inside. He smirked slightly and nodded. I pushed in.

The place was mostly empty. It was still short of five o'clock, and most civilized folks were at work. Alonzo always sat in a corner booth he deemed the Don Spot, where apparently he could see the whole bar, including all exits and bathrooms. It made him feel cool to imagine there would actually be someone out for his head. I didn't indulge his fantasy, sliding into the booth without looking around first for threats.

"Paulie! My man." He immediately started gabbing. I cut him off.

"Alonzo. Who are your friends?"

"How rude of me. Paulie, meet Natasha and Missy. Coupla girls from school. What perfect timing."

Alonzo went to a private school. The girls were wearing different shades of lime green miniskirts and flowery blouses, and were maybe a year or so older than him, but fluttering mascara-clotted eyelashes whenever he pulled out a money clip or ordered something expensive. I took a sip from Missy's—or Natasha's—drink. Fruity. Weak. "Let me get a whiskey," I said, when the waitress turned a polite smile my way. "Just fill it up."

"Paulie, something wrong? You quit your day job or something?" Alonzo looked at me from under a handful of Natasha's—or Missy's—hair and laughed.

"Yeah, I got something to tellya. Girls, go dance."

The girls frowned at Alonzo like I'd just introduced myself as Charles Manson's ambitious nephew.

"Hey, don't look at him; look at me. I said go *dance* a minute. Fuckin' go, or you're outta here."

They slid off the vinyl and rocked a self-conscious disco out of earshot from the table.

"Man, you know I could've had *both* those girls if you hadn't shown up? Now I gotta share..."

"Alonzo, I don't care about that. Listen, I might be wanted."

"Yeah, I'm wanted too. Those girls want to blow me both at the same time, right here under the table."

"They're sluts, Alonzo. That's what sluts do."

"Yeah? So?"

"So, I'm trying to tell you, I think I might've killed a guy today."

He coughed into his drink.

"Whaddya mean, 'think'?"

"I mean," I rasped, leaning close, "I didn't exactly stay around to check his goddamn pulse."

"The junkie...?"

"No, this was just some guy I knew who fucked me over when I was little."

"Yeah?"

"Yeah. And I beat him real bad. Like outta control, y'know what I mean? I was mad," I added as an afterthought.

Alonzo grinned. I should have been surprised.

"What was it *like*? Blood everywhere? Weird gurgling noises?"

"Okay, you're a sick fuck, y'know that?"

"What are you going to do?"

"I went to talk to Don Aberto about it, but fuck that restaurant. It was way too busy."

"Yeah. There's some kind of event thing going on there."

Then two of Don Aberto's henchmen approached the booth.

"Gaeta," barked one. "Up. Let's go."

"What the fuck?"

"Hey kid—just do what he says," crooned the other. "The Boss wants to see you."

Alonzo stared wide eyed, nostrils flared and head tilted back. Being summoned by two thugs like this, after leaving the restaurant in a huff, did not bode well. I walked ahead of the goons, passing the cocktail waitress with my whiskey on a tray.

"Just put that on Alonzo's tab," I managed to growl past the lump in my throat.

The Don smiled when he greeted me at the front of his restaurant.

"Follow me," he said, leading me past red velvet wall curtains and a crowded waiter stand, pausing to greet and smile along the way. The clatter and steam of fresh plates of pasta, meat, and fish hammered down on me, and I remembered the sack lunch I'd left behind at work.

"You know why all these people are here?" he asked after a while. "They're here for a fundraiser for peace. This foreign war is hurting my business. Maybe I should get into gun-running."

Don Aberto led me past the swinging kitchen doors to a table hidden from the sight and sound of the main floor, exposed only to the shining, helter-skelter kitchen. The chef's table. For the I-est of VIPs.

"Now, Mr. Gaeta. What was so important it couldn't wait for after business hours?" His voice was calm, smooth and dry like the skin of a rattlesnake.

I spoke evenly and steadily, with no trace of a stammer.

"I might have killed a man today. I wanted your advice."

He looked at me, revealing nothing, eyes neutral.

"Care for a bite? Veal?"

My brows knit for a second. Confused. Then I nodded. "Yeah. Sure."

He murmured something to someone, and before long we had two juice glasses and a squat bottle of chianti between us.

"How did it feel?"

How to explain? The idea had been burning my brain for so long, imagining, picturing, dreaming, wishing for that moment. I'd imagined his eyes flaring in terror, before going dark forever. I'd seen his blood splashing, pumping, draining. I'd pictured stab wounds and bullets and baseball bats and axes and car bumpers and gasoline. I'd longed to have my hands on him, to get his neck in range of a blade. To beat him with my mop until only a mass of organic garbage was left over. To tie him to a cinderblock and roll him into Boston Harbor.

"Nothing. It felt like nothing."

"Nothing?" He raised his eyebrows.

"I mean," I hesitated, rubbing my forehead. "I mean, I felt angry and pumped *during*, but then after I felt nothing. Not even guilt. Just tired after the exhilaration and scared about getting caught."

He waited to speak until after the waiter set down a tray of cutlets. I eyed it, and looked up.

"I'm not really hungry, I guess. I'm not sure what I am."

"Shut up and eat, kid. You've been through hell today. That takes energy. Eat!"

I obliged. The veal was rich, light, juicy, surrounded by roasted peppers and garlic. It filled my mouth with flavor, tasted like a single cloud over a vineyard, the warmth of a sun-soaked rock, the feel of a cow huffing steam in the morning. I'd been nowhere near Italy, but it suddenly seemed as if I'd been born there and had just returned after years of exile. Turned out I *was* hungry.

For the moments I spent chewing, I forgot everything.

Don Aberto knew exactly what I was thinking.

"Good food is a form of meditation," he said. "It's a way of clearing your head of what's getting in the way."

I looked at him.

"You could be very valuable to me, with your flexible conscience."

"Flexible?"

"Well," he chuckled. "Forgiving, anyway. More wine?"

The guy sounded crazy, but the cup or two I'd gulped along with the meat made everything seem fine.

"Now tell me." He rested a hand on my forearm. "Who was this *scarafaggio*, and did he have any friends who might miss him?"

All of a sudden, without intending it, I took a step up the ladder. I watched Don Aberto talking about pig farms, industrial incinerators, acids, and woodchippers;

explaining contracts and honor among thieves;
speaking almost reverently about Dick Nixon as if he
knew the guy; indicating large stacks of money and
criminal hierarchies—waving his hand on and on and
on, weaving a spell over me with his words.

A door was opening, and the room behind it smelled
like silk and gun oil. Who could blame me? I dove right
in.

ooooo

Picking at my tiramisu, I chance a glance at the door.
Shadows. Frenetic movements. Menus falling.
Holly brags about the BMW she just bought.
Hostesses and maître d' shrink back in horror.
Guests murmur on, unaware.
Holly talks about getting her license.
A burst of sunlight.
Pots and pans and orders banging from the kitchen.
A heaving shadow, a coral reef of hair.
RRRROOOAAAGGGGHHHHH and I'm on my feet,
chair clattering behind me.

Holly shrieks as I throw my napkin down on the
table.

Shoulders back.
Arms up.
Toes.
He bursts through the maître d' and pounds across
the floor toward my table.

PPK yanked from its holster at the small of my back.
Hollow-point parabellum round chambered. Safety
disengaged.

Aimed steady.

I'm going to shoot this fucking Tongan. In the nuts.

Ruin his day and save my own. A sore groin for a sore loser. And if he never gets better—fuck him. Tempt the devil; get burned. He'd probably even prefer to get capped in the head. I know *I* would. But he doesn't deserve that kind of mercy. Plus I'm *not* risking a lifetime bid or the gas chamber unless I absolutely have to. A shattered pelvis could be excused in court as self defense. An emptied clip in the chest and face—not so much, no matter how good it might feel. Not to mention bystanders and collateral damage.

Diners cower as he races over, slapping away trays and glasses, and screaming like you wouldn't believe.

Three more feet, and he's crippled.

Two more after that, and he dies.

I'll take a second chance. But not a third. In my world, that's the seductive line between getting rich and dying. He doesn't give up after losing his jewels, he takes one in the face.

Almost there. And...

Bang! a busser tackles his legs, rolling him to the ground and knocking over two tables in the process.

I sit back down and lay my gun on the tablecloth in front of me, chewing on a toothpick and glaring at anyone who looks my way.

Holly sits at the edge of her seat, clutching the corner of the table.

"Okay, what the *fuck* was that?"

"He must have followed us after we left the compound."

"Is this the kind of thing that happens at these events?"

Never. This is bullshit. This shouldn't be happening. Out here, in a restaurant beyond the perimeter of the corporation's land, getting rid of a body isn't as easy a thing.

A self-defense investigation would expose all sorts of things I'd rather keep quiet. It would take political persuasion to keep my ass out of prison.

I'd be hung out to dry if I killed this man.

I'd be dead if I didn't.

Luck only lasts so long. Thanks, mister busboy.

"Hey, let's get out of here," I say, standing up and grabbing Holly's elbow too roughly, to keep my hand from shaking.

She kicks her chair back and scoops up her Louis Vuitton bag.

"Where?"

"Let's go for a swim at the hotel."

We brush off the apologetic maître d', who's bowing and scraping and offering all sorts of amenities, and into the cool summer evening as two cops on motorcycles rumble up to the entrance with sirens flashing.

A cab drops us off at the five-star hotel booked by my fighting contact—"agent," as he likes to be called—and we get up to my room.

Holly closes the door and draws the chain.

Safety.

ooooo

Is there anything worse than a broken daydream?

The clang of a prison cell.

The bray of a car horn.

A young man's body dangling from the teeth of an excavator on a ranch in the middle of nowhere.

Hearing your son grow up through a semi-rigid phone cord.

"Gaeta!"

A three-second verbal warning before another inmate stoops into your cell, product of a recent slew of in-cell murders, suddenly transforming your space into a shrieking klaxon of nerves and wariness.

Fists ball up.

Shoulders hunch back.

The room becomes a chessboard. Pieces and strategy: Bolted-down bed. Thin mattress. Blanket. Flimsy plunger. Sink knobs. Chessboard. Bookshelf. There's a shard of a broken plastic door hidden in a roll of socks, honed on cinderblocks and wrapped with athletic tape, transformed into a shank.

The bar of soap tied in a tube sock sitting at the edge of the sink is the best bet. Be prepared. Always.

"Who the fuck are you?"

A tall slender boy stands in the doorway. He should be stroking a guitar or playing tennis somewhere.

"Mr. Gaeta, can I speak with you?"

"Absolutely not. Get out."

In this prison, your door is open and welcoming between lights-on and lights-out. In contrast to a supermax joint, this is called Freedom.

"Can I show you something?"

"Fuck no. Get out of my cell. Or I'll throw you over the balcony, or beat you to death where you stand." He hesitates, noticing the sock/soap sap.

Then this motherfucker turns around, uncinching his jumper, and bends over, spreading his cheeks.

"Son, what the fuck are you doing? Get outta here!"

"Gaeta, listen," he says.

The homeboys are after him, he explains. They want to gangbang that ass, and keep him around as a sort of ragdoll playtoy. Can't really blame them: the kid is bronzed, hairless, young, fresh. Someone who likes sticking his cock where it doesn't belong to show off his power and get his locked-up rocks off would get a kick out of this kid who would fit better on a college campus.

Out of all the fish, the white-collar guys are the ones who get it worst. It's like some kind of revenge, a way for the lower class to get back at the upper class when the playing field is leveled and they're all crammed together in the same concrete and cast-iron world. Ten guys would pass him around in a circle, and have enough time to recover and pass him around again. Before breakfast.

"This can all be yours," he says, smacking his right butt cheek. "All yours, whatever you want to do, as long as you save me from those guys. Can you imagine what they'll do to me?"

Sure you can. Live here long enough and you learn the ropes. This is why the first thing you do when you arrive in a new prison is scope out the world you've just been born into. And then you make your mark. Beat the hell out of some young tough. Demonstrate that you may be new meat, but you're strapped with gristle and experience.

Now, this isn't always such a simple thing. Stripped of the normal trappings of society, the only bonds inmates can forge are along color lines. If you're a white guy, you don't go looking to thrash a spic or a nigger unless you've got your own posse to back you. Same if you're a black guy—you can't tear off an Aryan's swastika tattoo unless you have the strength of the Crips in your shadow.

But if you waste no time displaying your independent grit, you become a potential asset to every group. Racial geography aside, everybody's looking for allies and assets. Or at least neutral types who handle only their own shit.

And so you rock some unconnected punk, and send him to the far reaches of the infirmary. You've got your rep. Now you're just holding onto the belt. If you mind your own business, and don't cause problems with groups of guys, and don't look into people's cells as you walk past, and don't get mixed up with drugs, and don't fuck somebody else's boyfriend or girlfriend, you'll be all right.

But despite all that, you still wake up every morning and don't know if you're going to live through the day.

Welcome to prison. You want to be the husband or the wife?

Hmm that's a tough one. Husband.

Okay, husband. Come suck your wife's dick.

The running joke among cellies. Ha-ha. Who's laughing?

If you're a tough guy, the system ain't bad. You sometimes have to tune a guy up, but you get left alone. You disappear. You've made it to the qualifying rounds, and it's time to rest up.

The kid is waiting for an answer.

"Sorry, buddy, I'm not interested. My sentence ain't that long. Maybe if I had six-hundred years...but you know. Why don't you just get outta my cell."

"But they'll kill me."

"Come on. What can I do for you, kid? This is prison." This is why you call in favors and spread bribes to get an unshared space whenever it can be arranged. There's really no question about throwing the boy to the dogs. Standing in the way of a whole gang of horse-dicks ain't exactly an adaptive behavior. More like suicide.

Most likely they'd just pass him around for a while and then ditch him for some new fish. They'd get bored. Savage as they are, they're only human. Nothing desirable stays that way forever. Once it's been touched, anything can lose its luster. And after being hollowed out and used up, the kid just wouldn't be worth a green light. Probably.

Killing someone in the joint, especially someone who hasn't offended the staff, is a sure way to stay here forever, and most of those hood-rats are only in for minor drug felonies or third-offense larceny, with the occasional armed robbery thrown in for effect. Kiddie gangsters like that may be stupid and blinded by pride, but at least they're able count twenty-five-to-life. They wouldn't risk that for a mere garbage disposal.

This piss-ant white boy might wind up afraid of shadows for the rest of his life, but he'll survive the bid. Probably. In for petty counterfeiting or making IDs for high-schoolers or something like that, first offense. Means he'll be out in 26 months. Probably.

It's just Time.

"You won't protect me?" His eyes glaze over.

This kid is only a couple years older than Dante.

Ignore that. Doesn't matter. Don't worry about it. Stick to yourself. Survive alone. Getting mixed up in something—well, if nothing else, prison survival is a matter of tit for tat. Karma. You put neutral in, you get neutral out. You put bad in...well. There's always someone worse than you, crazier than you; someone more willing to die than you.

The guy who gives less of a shit always wins the fight.

Shake your head. Fuck it.

Kick him out of the cell.

At the doorway he stops. Turns slowly.

Fists clench. Breath quickens.

"Mr. Gaeta," he says, polite like a snake. "It's not that simple."

"The fuck you talking about?" The way his whole demeanor changed. Like some sinister cartoon.

"The Delaney Brothers know I'm here talking to you."

"So?" The air in the cell suddenly feels heavy and inescapable, like trying not to fall asleep at the wheel.

"So, there's rumors going around that I'm riding with you."

In other words, your prag. Your bitch. Your girlfriend. This fucking kid.

"What d'you mean 'rumors'?"

"It's just what people are saying." He shrugs, somewhere between smug and apprehensive.

The deviant little piss-ant. He told them. Fucking serpent. Already announced his protection. Should wrap his neck around the flagpole in the yard. Should drown him in the washing machines. Melt him in the welding shop. Tell the Aryans he's got a meth-using gay black lover at home who's raising an illegitimate son as an atheist.

But the homeboys still want his tight little hole, which means he's also protected by those who want to ravage him for themselves. Because now he's stolen property. Infringed-upon territory. Based solely on a speculative lie. If he shows up defaced or dead, they'll see to it that whoever's responsible winds up in the morgue, and then take him for themselves. It's become a turf war, and he's turned himself into prime real estate for guys who have nothing else to care about.

Gangbangers like that don't understand reason. Their brains don't follow logical trails. They smell *dishpect*, and they're up in arms. They hit the mattresses, as the Don's guys used to say. War. In their tiny little raisin brains, this tanned young suburbanite is *theirs*, and anyone stepping on their toes or ruining his pretty, fuckable face winds up wearing a target.

Turns out it doesn't even matter if you want the kid's snatch or not. It's become a matter of death or live another day. Completely trapped; pushed across the board like a pawn. Skillfully manipulated. Forced into a diagonal choice between kill or die.

In other words, buy a turn. Buy some time.

Fucked if you do, fucked if you don't. Should've seen it coming.

Welcome to prison. Shit—welcome to life.

It's only a matter of time.

ooooo

"I always wanted to be a vet or a zoologist when I was little," Holly says, sparking a cigarette and pulling a sharp drag. "Just like any little girl," she adds in a smoky whisper.

"Well, you *do* take care of a bunch of animals..."

"Yeah, that's true," she laughs.

She coasted through the first years of boarding school with no real interests. Everything was sunny and perfect: a boring, charmed life of studying for math tests and secret notes passed between desks, and sneaking down the redwood tree outside her dorm window at night while her mother sat at home playing mahjong and smoking cigarettes with the neighbors.

Then her mother found the baggie of pot in her duffel when she was home for the holidays.

I know what you doing, she'd said, wagging a finger. *You want to smoke these weeds? You want to take this life I given you and throw it out with the bathwater? Fine. Pack you things.*

There was no arguing with a Chinese mother after she'd made a decision.

What do you mean, pack my things?

I not sending you back to that school. You know how much I waste to send you there?

But Mama, all my stuff is at school. I have to go back.

You violate this country laws? You not want to live here? Pack.

So she packed. She packed what she had, and the few things she'd left behind; old tired hairbrushes and faded t-shirts and too-tight 501 jeans. She didn't know what else to do.

Why am I packing?

Beijing.

Why?

Her mother picked up the phone and rang a taxi for the airport.

Then another terse phone call, in staccato Mandarin, shrill and loud over the long-distance static.

A long silent ride to LAX. Clearing security—Mama bowing and scraping for the uniformed high-school dropouts frowning into bags and scanning for weapons.

A plane ticket thrust into her hand.

Seats in the back near the toilet.

Chain-smoking passengers with shaky drinks. A slow lurch forward.

A stomach-wrenching tilt and buildings like matchboxes, roads like flannel patterns.

Next stop: Beijing.

ooooo

News, like disease, spreads with a speed directly related to proximity. Packed in like sardines, inmates pass on everything from meningitis to sports scores to yawns. And, in the proverbial game of Operator, information tends to magnify and distort as it passes.

It couldn't have been difficult for this kid—Shaun—to get the rumor spread. This place runs on the power of suggestion. The more insecure a person or group is, the quicker they jump at any threat.

Your very existence now threatens to take away a bit of meat from the circle of bull fags who want his o-ring, which must mean he's extra desirable. People always want what they think someone else has. Suddenly, your quiet hunkered-down lifestyle is over, and you're a Public Enemy within a zipcode of public enemies. Bad news.

He can't just be given back, either. There's no Sorry, Just A Big Misunderstanding in the joint. Sloppy seconds with no conquest would be considered a slight.

"Gaeta!"

A shadow steps into the cell.

"Who the fuck are you?"

The short black man says nothing, but lifts a paperback *Death in the Afternoon* from beside the sink.

"Hey, buddy, this ain't a fucking public library. Can I help you with something?"

He flips a few pages.

"Mr. Gaeta, you familiar with the Delany Brotherhood?" He speaks in clipped syllables, like a professor.

The Delany Brotherhood is a motley gang of black-nationalist cons with a half-baked philosophy and an over-cooked notion of the respect they deserve. Sort of a cross between Malcolm X's redheaded bastard stepsons and common schoolyard bullies out to steal your milk money. But they're also the most dangerous group Inside at the moment.

"Yeah, of course I've heard of 'em. You know that. So what?"

"Mr. Gaeta, there a count in thirty minutes, so I'll make this brief."

"Yeah, do that."

"The Delany Brotherhood want that boy," he explains, jerking his head toward something vague, "and you taken a piece of tail away from them. You upset the balance in this facility here. That's bad."

"He offered to be my prag. I said no. I'm not trying to get involved in anything political here."

"Oh you already involved. Like it or not. But I can make the Delany Brotherhood go away."

"Oh yeah?"

"Yeah. *And* you get to keep the boy."

Arms spread: How?

He explains that the leader of the Brotherhood owes him a massive favor. He could call it in.

"Yeah? Why would you help me? What do you get out of this?"

"Your boy Rosen. Marty. The Jew heroin guy from the Bronx. You friends with him, right? Introduce me to him."

"You're not his type."

He smiles, white teeth beaming through his face, ignoring the quip. He wants Marty's business savvy, not his companionship. Rosen is something of a legend in heroin circles, and this guy probably thinks he can get rich quick with a connect like that.

Without a go-between, these two junk slingers would never come in direct contact. It's general knowledge that Jews hate niggers, and black folk hate fags. So this is just an opportunist trying to initiate an unlikely but lucrative business partnership.

"In exchange for your glowing recommendation, I be willing to use my favor plus a little cash flow from the smack to convince the Brotherhood to lay off you. But you might still get problems from his cellie. Who happens to be they soldier Big J. He want the kid personally." He spreads his arms and shrugs. "But I can convince the *rest* of the brothers to let that stay a personal one-on-one between you and him. They business-smart. Money trumps beef. You a fighter, I hear. Should be a piece of cake."

The championship round. That old familiar surge, power reserves kicking up and rumbling to the surface once again.

"Fine. Fuck'im. Bring him on."

The only problem is, Big J is a monster, stacked at nearly seven feet and well over three hundred pounds. He's a giant of a former defensive tackle who snapped in a bar one night after losing his scholarship, and murdered two guys. He's killed at least one guy Inside too, and he's probably never leaving the grounds, except in a custom-sized body bag.

A guy with nothing to lose. God alone knows why they haven't moved him to a supermax joint. Politics. Welcome to Affirmative Action, filtered down through the system where it doesn't even make sense. The screws all hate him, and each of them privately wishes it was forty years ago when they could have just beaten him to death with nightsticks, with no serious consequences.

He's the kind of guy you'd pull a strap against if you chanced to come in contact with him, the kind of guy who wasn't even allowed in the bare-knuckle circuit because his size meant he could never pull enough odds to make gambling worthwhile. The kind of guy who was legally supposed to get an extra portion of food in the cafeteria because he needed more calories to stay alive.

They should reopen The Rock and stick him in the hole.

And then fill it with dirt.

Piece of cake. Right. Against a guy like that, the fight would inevitably end in death on one side or the other. Hyped-up bulls like Big J don't stop till they're in the ground. Which would mean time in the hole and loss of privileges at best for the winner.

But even though he outweighs you by the better part of a hundred pounds, and his fists span your face, and he was sucking tit when you won your first fight—the secret is, he's overconfident and has never needed true skill. His weapons are size and intimidation, and it's not hard to get past both. No matter how big he is, if you can slip inside his guard and catch him solid on the jaw below his ear, he's going down. And once he's down, he's done. It only takes a few seconds bouncing between fist and floor. Plus you can bet the C.O.s wouldn't be too quick to break it up—they'd even probably testify self-defense.

But if he catches you halfway, he'll paint the concrete with gray matter. If he swings first, his wingspan could make all the difference. If he's had any kind of training, the odds change. The balance is already in his favor. Fight him alone or else fight him with all his shank-happy buddies.

What a choice. Death or solitary.

"Wants the kid for himself, huh? C'mon, let me introduce you to my neighbor. Let's see what he thinks about your little gift."

Twenty minutes till count.

Walking a pace behind him, strolling down the unit toward Marty Rosen's cell. The guard at his post barks, *Rosen!*

"Heyo, Rosie, how's it hangin'? This is—"

"Please allow me to introduce myself," cuts in the professor. He explains his position and his business prospects, and apologizes for foreshortening the personal recommendation. For the sake of politeness—as well as not getting more involved—it's best not to listen to the business talk. Better to concentrate on setting up the pieces on Rosen's chessboard for the afternoon match. Then the bell rings for count, and it's time to go.

Done and done. Here goes nothing. Here goes everything.

ooooo

After landing in China, Holly was taken to a small brick house on the outskirts of Beijing. Mama and Great Uncle chattering in rural Mandarin so she couldn't really understand, beyond a few words like *trouble* and *ungrateful* and *teach* and *wife*. The sizzle of fish from the wok in the central kitchen. The smell of garlic and peanut oil.

What time is it?

What day is it?

How do you say *bathroom*?

Great Uncle frowned at her bouncing foot to foot and flapping her hands, and asked, in precise Mandarin so she could mostly understand, if she'd been brought up without an understanding of politeness.

I must go, she responded, looking down and squeezing her legs together. Great Uncle's jaw dropped, and he led her to the toilet, while her mother buried her face in her palms.

Mama spent a week chatting with the various relatives in the area, advising Great Uncle on selling his jade closer to the tourist hotels, and venerating her ancestors stuck in their homeland.

Then she left.

Holly awoke one morning and found herself alone. She sat through breakfast with Great Uncle and Great Aunt, saying little and nodding to their questions. They behaved as if Mama hadn't just up and left, leaving her behind in a place a million miles from home. Eventually she realized there was nothing she could do, no way to fix the situation. So she went along with it.

She followed them to the countryside to visit the relatives, and she sat polite and quiet the whole time, like a good girl ought.

She ate the food and drank the water and prayed to all the right dead family members, and let her hair grow until the braid reached down her back, and learned the language as best she could.

She stayed in whenever she wasn't out with Great Aunt, and spent time drawing flowers with charcoal. Her education took place at home at the kitchen table with few ratty books from the library. She wasn't even allowed to talk to the rickshaw drivers when she went into the city with Great Aunt.

It was four months before Mama called. By then Holly had grown accustomed to China and the visits to the country. She still had no friends—it wouldn't have been easy even if Great Aunt hadn't kept her in her sight all the time—but she soon felt the calming benefit of accepting her solitary life. No drama. No boys. No grades to keep up. No parties.

At first the absence filled her with tension until she had to slice her skin to keep it from exploding. But over time her drawing improved, and she put more and more of herself into it until she found release in the *shh* of the charcoal and the heat of fingertips rubbing shadows. One day Great Uncle even brought home a set of paintbrushes and some gloppy paint.

But no canvases. So she painted a mural of birds on branches in the converted closet that was her bedroom, birds with legs stuck in the bark.

Great Uncle noticed and strode in with fire in his rheumy eyes, but when he looked at the painting his face softened after a few moments, and he drifted out of the room stroking his beard, lost in thought.

A few days later he came home after selling his jade and presented her with a stack of canvases and a bundle of better brushes—almost as fine as the ones used for writing in the schools.

ooooo

The kid doesn't go out for recess. When everyone else goes to the yard for some fresh air, he stays in the library and tries to go online. The hacks usually let him. They're pretty well aware of what's going on, of who's interested in what; a result of being confined most of the day behind the same bars as the cons. Walls have ears, and that sort of thing.

It's hard not to shuffle in oversized sweatpants and Crocs.

"Hey, kid."

"Shaun," he suggests, not looking up.

"What, you don't look a guy in the eyes when he talks to you?"

"Sue me."

"Listen, punk. You're a fucking sneaky bastard, and I should make you eat this computer, but I respect your game. You win. Now be the lady and act polite. Because even though you set this up perfectly, it's on you to make sure I'm nice and cozy. Cuz without me here, you're even more fucked for trying to sneak around those Delany boners."

He turns slowly and puts on a smile. "I know you'll find a way. I've heard all about you. No one wants to mess with you."

"Yeah, well now they do, thanks to *your* ass." Clap him on the shoulder like a son and match his smile. "Which reminds me. There's someone I want you to meet."

In prison time itself has no consistent meaning: days stretch on into eternity, while years whirl down the drain. The Outside World changes, and only glimpses get through the bars, like clicking through one of those View-Master things with the disk of slides. Cocaine used to be the popular drug. Now it's heroin again. We used to watch our B-rate movies on VCR. Now they're on CD. They offer a choice between phone and email nowadays—but they still read everything and censor it the same.

What's Inside doesn't change much. The walls may get a new paint job every so often. The hairstyles get longer or vanish; the music and TV stations play different garbage; the Yard Baseball jerseys get new trim colors. But it's all more or less the same. Which means the only source of excitement is ownership. In a place where there are no private possessions in accordance with Federal law, ownership means varying degrees of slavery. Pounds of flesh.

Leaving the kid with Rosen leaves time to think. This way, at least someone will be getting some ass. And at least this little fuck will still get what's coming. Rosie will have him in makeup. He'll have him unable to sit down. He might even lend him out to anyone looking to score. Sure as shit hope so.

It doesn't matter that you're too old to stand an even chance against Big J. There's a fine line between what you gain from experience and what you lose in physical sturdiness. It's a savvy fighter who knows all the weapons available to him—position of the sun to control an opponent's vision; a slight rise in the ground that could trip him up; the noise of whoever's watching; a trivial limp from an old sports injury; left-handed versus right-handed—there are so many factors to keep in mind. Anything can become an advantage. And any advantage can even the odds. Experience means cunning means deception means exploitation means winning and walking away. Devour to survive.

Rally around a cause. Focus.

Anticipation like a drug.

A goal, a promise to live for.

What could be better than defeating a fighter half your age? Anyone watching would see the flicker of a grin hovering around thin-set lips.

And a shadow deepening under jaded eyes.

Drop and bang out twenty pushups.

Thirty.

Fifty.

Eighty.

Tug the mattress from its bolted-down frame and fold it into the corner of the wall.

Jab.

Jab.

Tentative. Lunge and jab, lunge and back again.

Left foot forward, right leg flexed like a coiled spring. The cinderblock walls crumble to dust. The shaft of light streaming through the window slit lashes out—duck away. Hop back and forth over the splash of sunlight, stiff ankles crackling as they loosen up.

Two hundred hops.

Thirty more pushups.

Lie on the floor, arms overhead, and sit all the way up. Fifty times better than crunches. Full range of abdominals. Full body engagement. See how many you can do. Right now.

Hang from the door bars. Pull up. Pull up. Pull up. Switch grip. Chin up chin up chin up. Leg lifts, knees-to-elbows, static hang.

This is how you wake up a sleeping dog.

Even at 49, you can whip yourself into fighting condition.

Legs outstretched like an L, heels on the concrete, hands on the bedframe. Down. Up. Poor-man's dips.

Body-weight squats, slow down; fast up. Arms overhead. Feel the quads taut against the skin. Explode!

Hopping over the shaft of light—fifty-five...eighty-nine...one-forty-four—closing eyes and counting until you lose track, a back-and-forth pattern of sweat droplets sprinkling the floor. Machine smell of iron and WD-40, clinking and grunting of exertion. The melody of blood flow. A symphony of focus.

Something to dance to.

ooooo

Holly pirouettes across the suite, skirt fanning out, apparently forgetting all about the assault in the restaurant.

"Damn, girl, aren't you too full to be dancing like that?"

I'm stuffed. I feel like I have mashed potatoes and filet mignon coming out my ears. At least dinner was free...

Sorry a maniac tried to kill you, sir. Your meal is on us tonight.

Great. Thanks. A lot.

"No way. I'm too ramped! Dance with me."

She comes toward me and curtseys.

"I need a bath," I say, shaking my head. "Wash me. Relax me."

She smiles and glides into the enormous suite bathroom to turn the water on. I flop on the bed and pinch the bridge of my nose with my eyes closed.

It's not supposed to be like this. Fighters aren't supposed to cross paths outside the compound. That's why they escort the loser away. Or bury him.

This close to retirement, with wads of escape cash stashed away, I can't help but play more cautiously. Fighting—or shooting people—in public is a sure ticket to the can. And that's not a place I ever plan to go.

As a servant of the Dark Side, you wind up in jail every so often, but always at some point while awaiting trial, your witnesses get scared or disappear, or a key bit of evidence gets misplaced, or the DA decides not to prosecute based on a technicality. This is life. When you're valuable, you're protected. Sleeping in county for a few days ain't like doing a bid. It's more like a really shitty motel room you can't leave.

Prison and jail are different like school and church. Either place, you don't *want* to be there, but you're stuck for a certain amount of time. In jail they leave you alone—you might be innocent. In prison, they shove things down your throat and keep at you like flies on shit.

"You coming in here or what?" Holly pokes her head out of the bathroom, wrapping a naked leg around the doorjamb and tousling her hair like an actress. A wrapped towel exposes her narrow shoulders and the light pulse in her neck. Classic. She flings a plastic-wrapped bath sponge at the bed, which I dodge easily, catching a glimpse of her towel falling off as she ducks back into the bathroom.

I strip off my shirt, dropping the cufflinks in the breast pocket, and unbutton my slacks.

In the bathroom before shucking my socks, I check the Walther's chamber and set it *click* on the marble countertop, covering it with a hand towel.

Holly stands on a ledge in the tub with her hands on her hips. Goosebumps spread up her olive skin as she settles into the water, and she absently traces her French-manicured fingertips up a neat ladder of scars on her thigh, moving to stroke a trim triangle of pubic hair.

For a moment I see Francesca, long dark hair, head tilted to the side, breasts full but not heavy—just how I'd design them. No waste beyond a good handful. For a second I'm sixteen. I'm seventeen. I'm in the Towncar when she borrows it without asking. I'm on day-off, under their pool table sprawled naked on a mohair rug. I'm huddled behind her shower curtain when her father comes home early, wrapped in a tiny towel waiting, still wet, shivering, freezing. Still hard as a rock.

"You okay?"

Holly.

The mirror is so big, I can stand back and it's like there are two of her in the water. I mount the steps and gingerly join her in the hot water, pushing mounds of bubblebath aside and sinking inch by inch to get used to the temperature.

"Ooo, wait," cries Holly, reaching over the recessed rim of the tub. She hands me a compact mirror with a few white lines on it, and a rhinestone-encrusted straw.

"You expect me to use this?" I ask, shaking my head.

"Okay, fine," she rolls her eyes. "Use this." She rummages a Benjamin from her purse and twists it into a tube.

"That's more like it."

I take the first two lines like I'm smelling flowers. It looks like magic, white specks vanishing an inch away from the edge of the bill.

I sit up and sniffle between my fingers pinching nostrils.

Machine-oil taste.

Numbing drip.

Hem!

The cadence of the lights.

The hush of bubbles on marble.

The *slop slop* of wavelets in the tub.

Her nipples bob in and out of the water, puckering in the air. The bottom edge of her hair clings to her neck.

I settle deeper into the tub.

Holly bumps a line. The gem in her nose glitters alongside the bejeweled straw.

The air conditioner hums.

A distant siren shrieks its way downtown.

Elevator doors clatter shut in the hall.

My reflection in the hand-mirror stares up, watching
with a twinkling eye as two more lines disappear.

Hot water soothes sore muscles.

A smooth leg drapes across my lap.

I flick the pedicured toes, trailing fingertips up her
shin to the knee.

She leans forward, offering a white-coated finger.

Open wide for the gummy.

Numb.

She pops the finger out and sucks it herself,
appraising through slitted eyes.

I say, "Wash me."

She leans forward, forearms on my shoulders, and
scoops bubbles with the sponge, squeezing suds down
my back.

"You're cute," she purrs in my ear. Her kisses taste
sweet, like a peach, and water sloshes as she adjusts to
straddle my lap. My hands slide to her hips, alternating
between a firm grip vaguely preventing her from
moving closer, and a soft acquiescence allowing her to
bear down.

She moans softly. "I don't normally allow guys to kiss
me..."

I reach up and take a handful of her hair, tugging her
head back and kissing her neck, collarbones, chest.
"Good thing I'm not a john," I remind her, "so you can
do what you like."

She opens her mouth to say something, but stops
with a shiver. Her breath catches. She arches her back,
thrusting her chest forward, smiling down and petting
the back of my head.

Fingers tangled in her hair, I pull back and look at
her.

"Look at you...god*damn*." Then I stand abruptly, still holding her around the waist as water rushes down our skin. Kissing her firmly on the mouth, I flip her upside-down and bury my face between her legs. She squeals, and then reaches for me, wrapping her legs around my neck.

After I set her down on the marble deck around the tub, eyes glittering and face flushed, she says, "What was *that*?"

"Surprise stand-up sixty-nine," I tell her. "My signature move. Fun, right?"

Holly rolls her eyes and laughs, pulling me by my ears toward her pussy, exposed and wet, legs spread, leaning back on elbows, feet propped on the marble.

Her eyes close, and she trails fingertips across her chest, stroking a nipple.

"Please..."

She lifts slightly off the marble, arching and writhing, head thrown back, lips parted, hips bucking a desperate primeval rhythm that ends right where it begins, in the cyclical magic of muliebrity.

I stand and wipe my chin, pausing.

A slow penetration, slipping in, pushing and pulling, pressing together, feeling and hearing and tasting and smelling and watching.

Her left hand gropes for something, eyebrows peaking. Words and sighs catch in her throat. Water splashes over the rim of the tub, sloshing onto a stack of towels.

Bubbles pop, crowding to watch, and she laces her ankles together.

"You...I..."

Kisses on chin, cheek, nose. Her eyelids flutter, breasts heaving as she moans and scratches, thrashing, spilling mounds of bubbles onto the tile floor.

She moves and turns around, and everything is soaked, splashed.

Holding her hips, pulling deeper, harder, catching a groove as she pushes back, rocks back, reaches back and presses fingers against herself, electricity rippling from the center to every corner, her asshole winking up as she moves; and she moans and purrs, sucking breath through her teeth and using her hands, involving her whole body as she feels it growing, reaching out, feels glistening, feels strong, feels like a goddess, feels bigger than her skin and bigger than this room, feels the ancient tempo, surrendering to it and embracing it and sharing it, bodies gathering, focusing downward, and she squeals and squeezes...

Your mind goes blank.

For an instant, everything shuts down, leaving an empty chassis. Higher consciousness forfeit. Senses unfiltered. Time and place forgotten.

She arches, holds the moment, trying to pull it as deep as it will go.

Bodies flag, relax, sag against each other.

"Oh my god," she cries softly, and sits down on the ledge, hugging her knees with a small smile on her lips.

I close my eyes and settle back with a sigh, enjoying the hot water.

She drifts toward me, and leans into the crook of my arm.

"Only two guys have ever made me cum like that," she whispers, kissing my jaw.

ooooo

It's strange the Christians don't get more up in arms about the prison system. With all their die-hard social values, you'd think they'd flex their sanctimonious muscles to fix what's truly broken. It doesn't make much sense they don't turn their political eye toward these hellish pits of inhumanity and spiritual abuse.

Especially when sodomy is involved.

Any salty fundamentalist would have a field day behind bars, preaching about Adam and Steve, and sins of the father, and all that sort of sacrosanct soapbox bullshit. It would be grueling, but don't such people spew on and on about being put to the test and triumphing over iniquity? Isn't it more glorious to save the most deeply damned?

But no, they'd rather go harass some hapless little teenager trying to stave off accidental motherhood and keep herself on track for a successful life. Why deal with hardened cons who might bring violence, when they could go after someone's defenseless little daughter, already half-shattered?

The most salvation there is in this little hell-on-earth is a chaplain whose job description is to straddle the boundaries of dogma, who mutters his scripts by rote and leaves as soon as he can, to beat the traffic. The real holy rollers don't spend much time trying to save people who are actually lost—at least not the ones who don't have a penny for the coffers. Or maybe they're just too terrified to denounce a cocksucker who's willing to murder.

What it comes down to is, you get bored real quick on lonely fantasies about girls you've known or wished you knew. The human brain has a long capacity for groin-tingling reverie, but at what point does that no longer cut it?

There's plenty of guys getting hitched to other guys in the joint, especially among the lifers. Where else can you find someone to whisper secrets to, someone to play out fantasy games with? Who else can be a confidant, or whisper *It's all okay* whenever the nightmares get too real and you wake up tangled in threadbare DOC blankets and sweat. Especially when you wake up *into* a purgatory nightmare.

If the Christians knew how many man-to-man marriages there are in the pen, they'd flip a shit. Especially on the guys who actually use a Bible for swearing their commitments. Can't blame those guys though: gotta cover your spiritual ass, whatever you do with it in the human realm. And anyway, with one hand entwined in another man's, and the other on a dogeared King James—wouldn't it stand to reason an omnipotent God would just strike the two grooms dead if He didn't approve? Or at least tweak their desires back to the Christian Standard?

It's a funny thing to get all fuddy-duddy about, given they worship a God who was so bored and lonely He had to create a bunch of imperfect people to play with; who would fear and glorify Him, make Him feel loved and respected, praise Him for descending and impregnating some poor betrothed desert wench with His half-human son when the shit hit the fan. A restless deity. Makes you wonder: is Jehovah just a nickname for Zeus?

If God feels the pang of longing, does He also get horny? Are the angels just a swarm of His illegitimate kids? What would He do if there were no women around and He needed to bust His holy load? Is God just an entity locked in divine solitary confinement, creating our everything from His own nothingness?

Maybe.

But that's a whole other story.

ooooo

I lean back to let Holly massage my feet, as she alternates between drawing on a menthol and gossiping.

"I lived with family in China for a year before I was able to get my way back here. I like it better here."

She kneads her knuckles into the balls of my feet. I groan as she puffs a lazy series of smoke rings toward the ceiling tiles.

"I'm glad I went, though, y'know? It was a good experience. Like formative. I think I'm stronger. And I know I can survive on my own, anywhere."

I nod. It's hard to concentrate on what she's saying, as the stress and turmoil of the day ooze out under her pressing fingers.

She came back to the States a year later, when she was nearly sixteen, without telling her mother. She arrived in San Francisco with the rest of the Chinese immigrants, extended family of Chinese already living in California, visiting and ingratiating, with the hope of outstaying their welcome and learning English.

Bloken Engrish. Flied Lice. She must have heard every joke there was in elementary school. And now she was back. And on the wrong side of the jokes.

Home.

But it wasn't the same—didn't feel the same, didn't smell the same, didn't sound the same. American traffic, American voices, American Dreams all sounded alien and sterile and metallic. There was no singsong Mandarin murmur. No constant ding-ding of rickshaws. The roar of cars was incessant.

She thought she'd be relieved to see faces that weren't Chinese, but now the color diversity seemed senseless and frightening. On her way through Customs, she struggled to string sentences together in English, and her American passport raised skepticism.

She was embarrassed. She was exhausted. She almost cried. With nowhere to go, at the termination of a plan that led her no farther than the airport in San Francisco, she lugged her bags into the nearest restaurant and sat at the bar.

"Help you?" offered the bartender.

"Pepsi please," she said, relieved and comforted by the presence of fountain soda.

"That's it? Just Pepsi?" He leaned toward her. His hair was swept back but it had fallen over his forehead in an arch on either side of the part. He raised an eyebrow and brushed his bangs back. "Here. Have a real drink. First one's on the house."

"Thanks," she said, watching him tilt a stream of rum into the glass.

"How was your flight? Here, a Cuba Libre."

"Long."

"Yeah, I know what you mean. Where'd you fly from?"

"China."

"Whoa, man, that's like," he looked down between his feet. "A long way."

"Yeah. I was there for over a year."

"Hey, welcome back. Excuse me." He moved off to help another patron.

Holly sipped the rum & coke and stared up at the TV playing a news segment at halftime. Someone important in the Middle East had been assassinated. She didn't recognize the name, but he looked stern, with squinty eyes and a bald head. Looked like Great Uncle.

She had to suck down the rest of the drink to keep back the hot weight of tears.

"Thirsty much?" The bartender leaned toward her, swiping at things with his rag. Holly pasted on a sweet look.

"Are you offering me another?"

A knowing smile crossed the bartender's face. "Sure."

"This keeps my mind off the problem of how to get to LA," she purred.

"LA? Why didn't you just fly into LAX?"

"This is where my ticket brought me. But then...now what?"

I shift on the bed to give Holly better access to my calves, and ask how she'd gotten a plane ticket, hoping to extend the massage as long as possible while she talks.

She wasn't proud of stealing Great Uncle's jade money. For weeks she'd been watching him return from the market, dividing his wads of yuan and stuffing one half in a jar and the other in an envelope for Great Aunt's groceries.

Then one afternoon when he went outside for his pre-nap pipe, she hurried over and emptied the jar, replacing it with crumpled bits of newsprint. Sweating and terrified, she ran out of the building with the bags she'd packed ahead of time, and down the block until she could hail a taxi for the airport.

Her Mandarin had improved, but she'd never work as a translator. Some words just didn't stick. "Take me to...to where...people fly, people leave. The sky," she fumbled, hoping she wasn't inflecting anything awkward or insulting.

The driver looked mildly amused in the rearview, and shifted lanes toward the highway.

"You visitor?" he asked in English. She nodded. They rode in silence for a while.

"Weesh airline today?"

Holly shrugged. "Any of them."

The driver frowned. "Okay. Air China good?"

She nodded.

The driver read her the number from the meter. She counted out the bills and coins, and ducked out of the car, tugging her bags behind. A doorman shuffled to open the entrance door for her.

A woman her mother's age with smooth skin, thick lipstick, and a tight bun of hair beckoned her to the counter. Holly pulled out the money and said, "Los Angeles."

"There is no flight to Los Angeles until after the weekend," she said with a firm smile. "I can put you on the next flight to San Francisco if you like. That leaves in two hours."

Holly nodded and handed over her cash and passport.

She tells me she hates flying, as she works her hands over my thighs, rubbing her way up to my lower back and kneading my glutes. I grunt in reply and try not to squirm as her fingers explore. I'm not a huge fan of flying either. I prefer my feet firmly planted.

Fortunately the flight was uneventful, except for a wailing baby right behind her that brought her to the verge of breaking down herself.

"So now that you're in SF, what *are* you going to do?" The bartender held a glass he was polishing up to the light.

"Huh? Oh, I don't know. Any good hotels around?" She swirled the ice in her drink.

"That's it? You don't have any family or anyone to pick you up here?"

Holly tilted the glass and chewed on an ice cube. "I sort of ran away."

"What, from China? Holy shit. I didn't know you could do that."

"Have you been to China? China's a hellhole. I grew up in LA."

"Can't say I have. I once went down to Mexico, though, back when I was in high school. We weren't supposed to go, but my buddy had a car—"

"Hey, I'm not sure this little lady is interested, chief. How about a Jack-rocks, big guy."

The bartender shot a fulsome smile at the suit-clad man who stooped to polish his cowboy boots before taking a seat. He was shy of forty with the air of a former athlete who'd not yet come to terms with a developing potbelly. A ready smile. Shoulders thrown back; head up. Standing like he was always on the verge of hooking his thumbs in his belt.

"See something you like, honey?" he asked, sitting down next to her.

"That depends on what I'm seeing," she said, surprising herself. The man's eyebrows lifted, and an amused smirk crossed his face as the bartender laid a glass on a cocktail napkin and heaved a rack full of dirty glasses toward the kitchen.

"What's your name, kitten? How old are you?"

"You have to earn my name," she purred. Where was this coming from? "And I'm eighteen," she added. "Duh...I'm in a bar."

"She's got spunk, ladies and gents," he laughed. "You've gotta give her that. I'm Eliot." He thrust out his hand, and they shook. "Where you coming from, princess? Or going to."

"China. From."

"No kidding. Fuckin' A." He raised his glass in a toast and downed most of it. "So what are you, visiting? or what?"

"Moving back to LA."

"No kidding. I'm on my way there myself, after a bit of a layover. When's your connecting flight?"

She didn't have one. Not enough cash. Apparently jade wasn't as valuable as she thought. Neither was the yuan. With about $25 and change in her backpack, what exactly she aimed to do upon arrival in the States was still unclear—but here she was. She felt stuck between two worlds, still not comfortable in America, but not exactly missing Beijing either. There was one thing she wouldn't do: she would not call her mother, even though she'd probably already heard from the relatives the latest evil her bad child had committed. The ancestors would not be pleased. Whatever. Better not to think about it. Suddenly she realized how hungry she was.

"Take a girl to dinner before you fly out?"

For a moment Eliot gaped, but nodded with amusement. "I'd take you to a good place in Chinatown I usually go to when I'm here, but you're probably sick of that. How long were you there for?"

She wanted a burger. With cheese. And fries. And a shake. And salt. And a Pepsi. And mashed potatoes. And fried chicken that she hadn't just watched walk across the yard an hour before. Anything, anything American that would fill her growling stomach and get her mind off picturing Great Uncle's kind wrinkled face drooped in disappointment when he discovered her theft and disappearance.

"How about a steak, honey?"

Holly nodded.

The bartender sullenly tallied up their drinks, and Holly gathered her two small bags. Great Uncle had sold the suitcase she'd brought to China within days of her arrival, following instructions from her mother. He permitted her to keep the valise, on account of the fact they'd be taking the occasional trip to visit sick relatives in the country. She'd stolen the little duffel the morning before she left.

Both bags were depressingly slack, and she swallowed a bitter lump of embarrassment. She didn't even have a proper purse, coming from China, where the Communists scorned material obsessions. Creeps.

Eliot took her hand and crooked it around his arm as they walked out the bar. An electric thrill spread from her fingertips. He was only a little taller than she was, but his suitcoat was soft and smooth, and warm to the

touch. The way he walked—so different from the men
she'd grown used to, the Chinese men of indeterminate
age and absent assuredness who'd come bowing and
scraping to Great Uncle in an attempt to secure her as a
wife without even talking to her first.

Eliot held the door open for her, and guided her into
a waiting taxi outside the arrivals lobby.

I tell her she's a lucky girl to be surrounded by
consummate gentlemen. Must be some kind of damsel
magnetism. She laughs in my ear and presses her
thumbs into my shoulders.

"How do you like it?" Eliot asked, "French? English?
Australian?"

"What?"

"Your steak. What's your style? Texas?"

She clicked her tongue. "Stop showing off," she
chided, hugging his arm and smiling up at him.

"You got me, sugar. I just want to impress you."

"It will take more than just a knowledge of meat."

"Oh yeah?" Eliot leaned forward and instructed the
driver. Holly watched out the window as people strolled
down sidewalks, sifted through garbage cans, dropped
dimes in parking meters, waited for trolleys; hurried
and dawdled. It was all just people, but so different
from Beijing. Even the concrete looked different. And
the smell—San Francisco reeked of sewer and asphalt
instead of pigs and bicycle grease.

The restaurant was dim, illuminated by a single
candle at each table—and quiet, forks clearly clinking
over the murmur of conversations. She tried not to paw
at the velvet curtains or the burnished brass trimmings

on everything. The staff smiled and mouthed pleasantries as they passed, and she caught herself bowing low. Stop. This is America now. No one bows to anyone here.

A steaming basket of dinner rolls appeared on the table as Eliot ordered a bottle of wine. She wanted to cram one in her mouth so badly, but didn't want to gobble food in front of Eliot.

Instead she tore off a half and picked at it whenever Eliot took a bite of his. She almost ordered a salad for her meal, but Eliot ordered for both of them when the waiter returned.

The steak suffered no such delicate treatment. She ate the entire 10oz filet, and left only a streak of mashed potatoes. It tasted so good, but part of her wanted to run to the bathroom and get rid of the weight in her stomach, totally unused to such dense food. And then Eliot insisted on drinks at a club he knew.

"But I don't have my ID," she apologized, trying not to panic.

"Sure you do, honey, you must've had a passport, right?"

"Um. Yeah. But..."

"But what? Drinks're on me."

"But...well, I'm not actually eighteen yet."

Eliot's lips pressed together, and he worked his jaw. "Well alright, when do you turn eighteen then?"

"December...of '83."

"Fuck me running!" He peered at her. "You serious?"

She nodded. Eliot sat back in the booth. He toyed with the fountain pen he'd used to sign the bill. She apologized, and he waved it off.

"So...almost sixteen?"

She nodded again, and reached across to touch his hand. His gaze met hers, and he squeezed her fingers.

"Let me buy you a ticket to LA. I hate to see a kid on her own like this. You're too pretty to be alone. It's a dangerous world." He held up a hand as she pretended to protest. "I travel all the time for business. I'm in this new program that gives points to frequent flyers. I won't take no for an answer."

She smiled sweetly. "If you insist, Eliot."

On the way out, he hesitated before putting a protective arm around her. The hostess bade them a good evening, and a light fog greeted them on the street.

"As it happens," he said, "My flight's not till tomorrow morning. I'm up in a hotel for tonight. You got somewhere to stay?" He fidgeted with a button above his belt. Then he stopped. He took her shoulders and bent his knees slightly so his eyes were level with hers. They darted back and forth, and then narrowed. He leaned in and kissed her, pressing her back against the brick building.

"Age is just a number, right?" he breathed, kissing her again.

Holly kissed him back, and then tentatively rested her hand on the back of his neck, like in the movies. She and her boyfriend had just started kissing when she'd been whisked away to the Far East.

But Eliot tasted better. And felt better. And knew what he was doing. And instead of football-helmet acne on his chin, he had a rough stubble she found distinctly sexy. Holly pressed against him, fitting herself into the contours of his body and doing her best to melt in his arms. It worked.

Just like it works now when I turn over on the bed, and she nestles her cheek against my chest after lighting a fresh cigarette. Holly knows how to fit an embrace, even as I drift in the limbo between listening and sleep.

Eliot groaned faintly and pushed away from her, flinging his arm in the air to hail a cab. It took several minutes, but he finally flagged one, and they rode in silence to the hotel.

"This place has a pool," Eliot mentioned casually when they arrived, trying to maintain his stoic coolness.

She didn't have a bathing suit. He probably didn't either. She hung back a half-step when he retrieved his room key from the concierge, looking down to hide a demure blush. Then they walked arm-in-arm up the stairs to his room.

Holly hadn't been in a hotel since she was eight on the trip to Disneyland. Eliot flung his suitcoat over the back of a chair and loosened his tie. She went over and helped him, undoing the buttons on his shirt.

Suddenly he backed away, shaking his head. "This isn't right. This is so bad."

She thrust out her lower lip and leapt at him, clawing his shirt off his shoulders, burying her face in his faint musk of cologne, kissing the hollow of his neck. Her heart was beating fast, but she felt calm despite the heat rising from her abdomen. She pulled him against the dresser, knocking over the ice bucket and its glasses, and dislodging a watercolor from the adjacent wall. She looked down at the splintered frame, and then back into Eliot's gray eyes.

"Now," she ordered. "I haven't done this before, but show me—like any time before. Show me what you do with women."

His breathing quickened to a pant, face flushed and eyes narrow. Holly watched his muscles tense, watched him tear off his undershirt, watched his chest swell, tugged at the soft curls.

He stepped forward, hands gripping her shoulders and pressing her against the wall. His breath ragged in her ear; a woody aftershave filling her nostrils and sending tingles down her ribs. She shivered when he pulled off her shirt and exposed her breasts.

He caressed her shoulders, arms, hips; traced his fingers across the even row of short scars on her thigh—and he said nothing. With dry lips he kissed her neck, chest, bellybutton; tilted her head back and kissed her on the mouth. She touched his chin, tugged his hair, and let him twist her toward the bed.

"Wait," she whispered. "I'm...I've...this is..."

Her first time. Embarrassed, she pulls away, retreats. He takes her hand. Whispers *shhh,* guides her head toward the pillow, black hair splashing out behind her. Rests a hand on her thigh.

Her first time. Even so early, it's clear she'll always be like this, always deceive every man she's ever with. She'll giggle and curtsey, and nod and look down demurely, and make him think she's madly in love, desperately lusting, but inside, deeper than where anyone can go, she's established a secret, a hideaway, a vault; where she exists in happy security, existing just to exist, delighted by the charm of her little castle.

You can tell she loves love; loves the attention and desire always aimed at her, loves the appeal of men, the acrid scent of the masculine desire, the tumultuous need of the male creature.

From them she derives her power. She's Morgause. Enchantress. Seductress. Feigned innocence and diminution. She'll be the undoing of any number of powerful men, and that—when she understands it—she'll love.

Perhaps seeing a hint of this, Eliot positions himself between her legs, holding himself above her narrow thatch of downy hair, aligning himself and taking a breath.

And then it's in—a sharp pain that bounces up her spine and pumps her full of adrenaline—and then it feels good, and she feels open, revealed, exposed to the world, no longer sealed up, and she screams *My God!* and it feels good, and it stings, and she laughs.

Suddenly he calls her whore, slut, pins her wrists alongside her head, bites her lip, presses his weight down on her, dominates. Presses, pounds, in and out, skin slapping on skin, hot and feeling, and she can taste it. He thrusts hard, overdoing it in his anxiety to prove himself, biting his lip, eyes wide. And through it all, from that place within, she controls, allows, guides, using her power to make him feel powerful, thrilling on his trembling chin and sweaty desperation.

Her body feels cold when he rolls off, skin prickling, exposed. Hips aching, breasts tender, throat parched. An emptiness between her legs.

It hurt less than she expected. Surprised at the lack of blood, she reaches down, touches herself. Her fingers come away sticky and slimy, and she wipes them on the bedspread, and touches herself again, feeling the heat, the slight throb, the rawness that wants more.

Far down on the street below the balcony, she hears car horns blaring in traffic, and someone yelling. A road crew works through the restful hours of night, tink-tinking away. She hears a siren tearing through an intersection.

And she wants it again. Wants to feel that power. Reaches down, wraps her fingers around his penis, thrills when it grows heartbeat by heartbeat in her hand, weakly nodding yes.

Afterward, she knows, she'll remember this moment forever. Afterward he talks, she listens; morning-after pill and secrets and his job; she notices and revels in his squirming, his nervous glances, the tingle of power when she strokes his palm. She can always say no. To anything.

ooooo

There's a funny thing about time in prison, in that it doesn't exist—or it does, but it's something more like one of those Dali paintings, where the clock numbers run amok in technicolor confusion, and the hands can't quite seem to make up their minds which way to point.

You lose track of where to look, of how to judge whether what you're seeing is reality; whether it's now or tomorrow, whether you're waiting for last week or next Tuesday.

You glance away and look back up, and it's three years later. Then look again, and it's yesterday.

Every way you turn there's something telling you what time it is—but there's no way to tell which is right. Or if there even is a right. It's like that old classic about the guy who stands up on stage and says *I'm lying to you right now.*

Can't be.

Whatever the case, time is a funny thing in prison. It dances around with no regard to logical linearity or consistency. It hurries up and takes forever.

Remember grade school when the teacher plays with cardboard clocks, trying to show how it goes from one number to the next? And how the hands would sometimes get hung up on each other, frustrating the teacher and making everyone giggle and fidget? Prison's like that. It's like someone did that, and then shredded the clock and scattered the pieces.

Dear Paul.

Most of the time you have no idea what day it is, and time is measured by lights-on, count, breakfast, count, work, count, lunch, count, activities, count, dinner, count, lights-out.

Hours drag ass, weeks flit by, and years tumble like rocks down a mountain.

I'm supposed to come see you next Thursday. But you and I both know it's best I don't.

You can't hardly feel it, but the world Outside is chugging past—out with the old, in with the new. You pick up bits of it: digital security cameras, CD players, email...but everyone you know who got out on parole or finished a sentence—and then wound up back in on some easy charge—mentions nothing about all the change, which means all that newness is the scariest goddamn thing there is. At least in here there's a routine.

Every time we talk, on the phone, through the glass, in letters, in my dreams, we always have problems I don't think we can ever get over, even when you get out. We're always fighting, even if we're smiling and acting friendly.

Prison is the worst kind of hell, the kind where you're running up a staircase and everything's aching; thighs, lungs, hands, eyes, throat, all burning; but there's something up there, something you have got to get to. Except every landing always leads to the foot of another flight of stairs.

We can't keep doing this. I've talked to Dante about it. He's OK. He understands. He'll still come see you some. And then when you get out, who knows? He's going to college. He's on full scholarship at Berklee. He's like you. Only smarter.

There was a book on the library cart once about the Dalai Lama and monks who could meditate so deeply they pull themselves out of the senses of this world, slowing their heart-rates to near-death levels, and existing only within their heads. They remove themselves from the pain and competition of the world, self-contained Beings who don't need food or water for impossible stretches of time.

If only you could do that in prison.

It's been too long. I've met someone. And he's supporting me going to school. I already finished half of my gen ed requirements. It was easy, you were right. I really hope you will be alright. I'm sorry I did this in a letter. I just thought it would be better for both of us.

There are lots of things to look forward to in prison. Commissary day. Recess. Ice cream. Movie night. Lice checks. Phone calls. Visits.

Looking forward to something can help pass the time and keep you going. But it can also make time crawl slower. And it can make it confusing, like when you dream one night you're buying toothpaste from the Commissary, which means it must be Monday, and you wake up and think it's Tuesday. Just two more days till the Visit. Then no one bothers to correct you till you're next in line and it turns out you're not on the Visitor List, and someone tells you it's just Wednesday and you have to wait one more day.

At least there's mail call.

Goodbye, Paul.

ooooo

I met Alonzo's sister for the first time after dragging Alonzo's hammered carcass home from the bar on his eighteenth birthday. She was hugging a sweater, reading on the stoop outside their apartment.

"Bit late for reading, isn't it?"

She glanced up and shook her head. Her dark hair shone under the porch light.

"Should I just leave him here? Or bring him in, or what?"

"Should've left him at the bar."

Alonzo blurted something and struggled away from me, stumbling against the brick wall and retching.

"He's really quite the charmer," I said.

She sighed and closed the book, putting on a pretty smile and looking straight at me. "You must be Paulie."

I nodded. I had seen her every so often—but never alone, and I'd never spoken a word to her. Alonzo would always get all pissy if I so much as mentioned his hot sister. Not to mention I was a bit intimidated by her father's relation to the Don.

But now Alonzo was crouching by the curb, spitting loudly. And her father was asleep upstairs, resting up before tidying the Don's legal affairs. For a dozen twenty-hour workdays each year, plus the occasional court date, their father enjoyed a generous salary and a rent-free townhouse as a courtesy.

"So you know me. I don't know you. What's your name?"

"Francesca."

We stared at each other while Alonzo muttered in Italian.

"So, what are you reading?" I asked lamely.

She showed me the cover. *Romeo and Juliet.*

"It's for school," she explained. "Homework."

"Yeah."

"You don't really know how to talk to girls, do you," she asked, setting the book on the step beside her. "How old are you?"

"Maybe I'm not trying to *talk* to you," I said, grateful to be offended instead of awkward. "Maybe I'm just being po*lite*. I'm here to take care of your brother."

"Come here," she said, patting the brick and nodding toward her brother. "Look at that prick."

Legs nearly touching, together on the stoop we watched Alonzo kick at a can, miss, and wind up on his ass. With a great effort he pushed himself to his feet, brushed off his slacks, and jabbered angrily at us.

Then he threw up on his shoes.

"Jesus."

He pulled out a handkerchief and stooped to wipe the patent leather, but vomited again, groaning with his head in his hands and squatting like a Chinaman, heaving and spitting, and breathing in short bursts.

"What a mess. Let's get him inside."

We each took an arm and guided him toward the big green door. A brass lion's-head knocker watched as we pushed him over the threshold onto the hardwood floor. Francesca kicked a runner aside.

"Dad will kill him if he pukes on that."

The foyer was tall, arching over a gaudy unlit chandelier. I bumped into an wrought-iron umbrella stand in the corner, as Francesca positioned Alonzo at the first stair. A huge mirror in a gilt frame reflected a portrait on the opposite wall. The effect was eerie and sinister. I have no idea why anyone would decorate like that.

"Hey—help," she barked, interrupting my drifting thoughts. I pushed Alonzo, and he shuffled up the stairs one at a time, step-step...step-step...step-step, head lolling, apologizing and thanking, apologizing and thanking—and now and then slurring an erratic insult.

After closing Alonzo's bedroom door, Francesca linked elbows and escorted me down the hall.

"Great teamwork. How are you getting home?"

"Maybe you could give me a ride?"

"Nuh-uh. I just toked up. Maybe you should just stay here."

"Maybe I should just walk."

She brought me into her room and sat me on her bed in the shadowy glow of her desk lamp.

"The couch in the den is comfortable. Shoes off."

I did as she said, and tried not to worry what my feet smelled like out of my boots.

"Here."

She held up a hand-rolled cigarette pinched between thumb and finger with a dirty, skunkish smell. Grass. I'd smoked it once or twice before, with the Puerto Rican landscapers I worked with, but never really got into it.

Alonzo never smoked it—said it crippled his ability to talk to women. And made him stupid. I told him *he* made him stupid, not the grass.

The Don always scoffed that it was grown by the government to control the Negro population. To keep them submissive and lazy and uneducated. If he ever caught his goons with weed, he had them tied up and beaten with plastic bags full of thistles and other weeds pulled from abandoned lots, and then marooned on the turnpike to hitchhike back. If they came and apologized, they got their job back with no second chances. If not, they wound up dead.

She relit it with a paper match and passed it to me, tossing the match into an ashtray alongside a smoldering cone of incense.

"Your folks don't mind?"

"Please. Think they know what this is? Total squares. Wouldn't recognize good grass if they were having a *picnic* on it."

I took the joint and puffed a bit, swirling the acrid smoke around my mouth and hesitating before inhaling it deep.

Francesca told me, "Hold your breath," and I did—until blood filled my face and stars drifted across my vision. My chest drew up tight around my lungs, and when I couldn't hold any more, I released the smoke in a torrent of coughing.

Francesca laughs.

I cough.

A feeling spreads from my chest, a soft decrease in gravity, welling in my cheeks and reaching across my forehead. An army of alien caterpillars caresses my skin. My tongue sticks in my dry mouth. My eyes narrow, and the light in the room channels around what I'm looking at.

I cough.

Francesca laughs.

She gets up and pops a tape into her stereo, touching the volume knob.

"You like music?"

I shrug.

"Listen to this. This is a Pink Floyd bootleg. My father brought it from London a few weeks ago. It's new stuff—the album's not even *out* yet."

She feeds me the roach again as white noise gives way to applause and cheering. I spin around. Strange music warbling from my left. Crowd noise filling the back wall of the room. The ceiling pressing down.

Francesca's light-brown eyes glitter as she squeezes my arm. "You okay? Have you never heard stereo sound before?"

I shake my head. The music warps around like a fever, making me vaguely dizzy.

"Look at you," she whispers, giggling. "You're concentrating so hard."

"What are you, like some kind of hippie or something?"

She shakes her head, looking hurt. "Do I look like a sunshine-bum? No, I just like good, weird music. It takes me away from here. It puts me in a place where people have more imagination. Less fear. More freedom."

She hooks a strand of hair behind her ear. Smiles. Wills me to understand her. "There's not really another way for me. Not until I can leave for college and see the world." An escape. The grass and the music. The rhythm and the flow. The beat and the tune, so different from her father's seriousness and her brother's bravado.

Underneath her punchy attitude, there's a sadness, a longing, a challenge. She pouts, seeing me staring, and shifts her crossed legs on the bed, sort of swaying with the music.

"What do you think?"

Except for the song about money, I'm not really into it, but the bass line thumps against my chest and swells in my ears.

I can see what she means.

Suddenly she looks worried, holds a finger to her lips—*Shh!*—and presses her hand over my mouth.

Cheeks a few inches apart, we stare at the door, listening to the hallway through the pounding of blood in our veins; not breathing, scarcely daring to blink, every on-edge fragment of awareness diverted to our ears, feeling the music around us, feeling our hearts beating in sync, waiting, expecting, longing to hear something—a radiator rustle, a car rumble past, a dog start barking—anything to break the quiet outside.

Finally Francesca's hand softens on my mouth. Her shoulders relax. She turns to look at me, and our noses are nearly touching.

"Pot really gets me," she whispers. I bite at her fingers. Her hand moves to my shoulder, eyelashes lower. A glint of teeth between parted lips and a look that screams, *Kiss me!*

She pulls away and sings with the tape. "See you on the dark siiiide of the moon!" Then pulls me into a kiss, twisting her fingers in my hair.

When I tell her I've never been with a woman before, she believes it, and moves into Take-It mode. Suddenly she's the official representative of her sex, the wielder of limitless eons of female power; suddenly she's duty-bound to awaken me, to destroy my ignorance of the female figure with its unknown depths and mystical fertility.

If I tell her I've never been with a woman before, it's only because the two or three before were only shadows compared to this queen.

I'm in love.

It became difficult to convince myself otherwise. Especially difficult when we were meeting almost every day; fucking two, three times every time because each time could be the last time.

Thrilling on the illicit, thriving on the giddy anticipation, thrashing around in the secret club that only she and I were in. Hushed, hurried interactions; the rustle of clothes louder than the words whispered, almost louder than the cries muffled by each other's mouths, nearly as loud as the pounding heartbeats in our ears.

I would go to work for the Don and sometimes be too brutal, sometimes too quick to jump on a guy—because if I didn't act early, there was more chance I'd get hurt and not be able to meet Francesca later on. The alternative was to quit the Don's business altogether, and I couldn't do that. I was growing attached to silk shirts and never worrying about what I had in the bank before deciding on a purchase. I couldn't let go of the glory of having a roll of bills in one pocket and a gun in the other.

If Francesca knew what her brother and I did for the Don, she never mentioned it—and I never brought it up. We both seemed to agree it did not matter, as long as we had enough space to shut out the rest of the world and delve completely into each other for at least a few minutes of each day. But even with that, connected as we were, I could never quite wrap my head around the music she always played, could never absorb that part of her. I could nod to the basic rhythm and the drums, but no amount of squealing guitar solos ever excited me or got my blood up. It bugged her more than she let on.

ooooo

It's a perfect day for a run. The sun shines through the clear fall air and a short breeze blows off the river. A few people are out with strollers or dogs, and one or two lounge on the docks in the sun. Other than that, no crowds; no one to get in the way. Just me and the slap-slap-slap-slap of my new All-Stars, the pounding of my heart, and the rush of my breath.

In. Out. In. Out.

Breath control is muscle control. Muscle control is body control. Body control is power. And people can read that in the way you stand, the way you walk, the way you talk, the way you dress, the way you react in a given situation. Surround yourself with muscle, and you rarely have to use it.

Slap-slap-slap-slap.

Unless you want to; and then you seek it out. I stop and stretch my legs on a bench donated by some puke from MIT.

Muscles burning with satisfaction, but crying out for more. Thud-thud-thud-thud. Blood pumps through ears. A gull sweeps down under the Mass Ave bridge, and I take that as a starter flag for mile seven, and sprint off. At this point it feels better just to keep on going.

In-out-in-out.

Slap-slap-slap-slap.

My head bobs to my own rhythm, and my legs piston toward the concrete, pushing off with each step to spring farther with each pace and stretch myself to the limit.

A tingling spreads from cheeks to chest, and down through belly, hips, legs, feet. The body disappears, replaced by—

in-out-in-out

slap-slap-slap-slap

thud-thud-thud-thud

—repeated until it becomes a mantra. When you do what I do, you have to be ready for anything. How often does a scumbag who asks for a shady, illegal loan have qualms about committing violence?

And that likelihood can be minimized by a sturdy intimidation factor. Walk in like an athlete, like a muscle-bound warrior, and the guy'll think twice before throwing his empty wallet as a distraction from the fire-poker he's swinging.

The trick is to anticipate. Watch his face, his hands, the position of his feet. A guy will give himself away no matter who, no matter when. It's just a thing of how fast you can find his indicators.

And then bring the violence to him before he has a chance to act. Reaction before the action. A reversal of physics. Break his hand before he can grab a bat. Kick him in the knee before he can throw a tackle. Snap his wrist before he can pull a pair of scissors or a bent knitting needle wrapped with duct tape.

Some of the people who take our loans are just ordinary desperate people, calling on gangsters to get them out of the hole they've been digging; people who've misrepresented themselves and lied to their friends, families, partners, clients, investors, bosses; people who can't score a legit loan from the bank, or who don't want any sort of paper trail for whatever reason. People willing to pay our exorbitant interest for a tax-free cash loan. People who've fucked up and don't want to admit it publicly. And some of them are real trash.

The Don doesn't run around forcing people to accept his protection. He doesn't do the Whitey Bulger thing, even though they do business from time to time. But he does look out for his own: a restauranteur in the North End whose wife goes under the knife; the Don'll help out with part of the business for a while, until the guy can get back on his feet. A bakery has a fire in the ovens that destroys thousands in property; the Don'll rig up a contract for cheap, fresh bread from a mass-production company so the bakery can distribute and keep business going until the insurance allotment pays off. A school faces a wrongful-termination suit from a guy who fucked the mother of a student in exchange for a grade; the Don'll pay the attorney fees and have the culprit stuffed into a buoy on the Charles.

Then the Don makes a friend for life; the Don's restaurant gets free bread forever; the Don's kids get into their first-choice colleges. There's something to be gained from every gift, and from people like those, the Don never asks for repayment. The Don collects favors.

But loans are different. Loans are for the scumbags who live day to day, blowing whatever earnings they have on crap investments or easy cons or gambling or chemicals or women. They're for prison widows and down-and-outs with *brilliant* business ideas and no credit lines. They're for the scumbags who will pawn their wedding rings to go play a midnight game of Blackjack because they saw a pigeon-shit splatter in the shape of a spade. They're for shortsighted liars who think it's a good idea to get a pocketful of cash Right Now, neglecting to remember they'll have to repay *that* money too. They're for the kind of people whose knees I don't mind cracking with a billiard cue. The kind of people who'd rob a convenience store to pay me, rather than see me come in their front door with a length of half-inch chain swinging from my fist, wearing a particular kind of grin I'm told is rather frightening.

But God help them if the Don is acquainted with the owner of the store they robbed. Then they'll see me anyway, but the look on my face will be much colder. The Don doesn't tolerate petty crime against civilians. The Don looks out for his own.

Fighting, like anything else, is a matter of practice. To make sure we're ready for loan business, Alonzo and I mob around Boston stirring up trouble, hoping to be caught off-guard and adapt—or else. It's the ideal job.

Of course, we really do it because we've come to love the rush, the pounding adrenaline we've been addicted to since the days of King of the Hill. Facing a pissed-off dude with a few too many drinks in him is like stepping into the arena under the lights, ready for the whistle to start the game. We're the star athletes. And everyone cheers on their favorite team, till the cops come around and everyone plays innocent.

But most people will avoid a fight, posturing heavily up to the last second, and then turning tail before the clash. Even the act of pushing the escalation to the point of a fight-or-flight decision is a challenge—and no matter how abrasive and patient you are, there are always the namby-pamby excusers and the flat-out pussies who just back down. And then there's no sport. Then it's just a beat-down on principle. And that's not fun. No one is impressed when the varsity guys beat up the freshmen.

One time I was at the bar with Alonzo, chatting up two advertising models who'd been giving out Budweiser t-shirts and running drink specials all night. Alonzo noticed another girl watching from a waist-high table near the wall, so he beckoned her over. When he touched her hair and smelled her perfume, the guy who'd just bought her a drink came over with fire in his eyes.

"What's going on?" he demanded, glaring at Alonzo.

"This beauty right here wanted to come join our conversation," Alonzo said. "So I let her." He wrapped his arm around the girl's waist.

"I just bought her a drink, man. She's talking to me."

"Oh. So, why'd she come over here then?"

"Alonzo."

"Shut up, Paulie. I'm talkin' to this guy."

"Alonzo." I leaned in and stage-whispered in Alonzo's ear, looking directly at the guy who was Alonzo's height but more thickly built. "Come on, man, it wouldn't even be fun to mix it up with this little Mick pussy. He wouldn't last ten seconds if he had his three biggest friends here."

"I tell you what," Alonzo mollified. "You fight this girl—what's your name, sweetie?—you fight Juliana, and if *you* win, you take her home with you, and if *she* wins, I'll let her take *me* home and have her way with me several times. How 'bout that?"

"Psh!" The girl rolled her eyes and walked away shaking her head, stopping near the restrooms. She watched Alonzo and this guy face off, almost nose to nose, both of them forgetting all about her as they swayed back and forth with arms half lifted like wings.

Only a good tipping point needed to throw the thing into chaos.

Then someone waiting for drinks at the bar noticed the brewing situation and hustled over. I raised a hand to stop him from getting closer, and he shoved my arm away.

"Move. That's my buddy," he growled, and tried to get past.

"Oh, you're with *him*?" I asked, grabbing his collar. "I can't have you throwing the odds off. Because *that*...is *my* buddy." I shoved him into his friend who panicked and flailed a fist, catching Alonzo in the throat. Alonzo retched, coughed, caught his breath, and threw a tackle into both guys, knocking them further off balance as the newcomer—who was bigger, more my size—tried to level a kick at Alonzo's ribs.

I shot a look at the blonde—Juliana—and shook my head in mock disapproval of it all.

Then I dove in.

Slap-slap in-out slap-slap in-out.

Pavement rolls toward my restless feet. Sweat streams down forehead, arms, belly, thighs. Chilled by the breeze. My breathing syncs with my steps, slap-in-slap-out-slap-in-slap-out, and my heart follows. I shadowbox as I run, reaching toward the enemy, the next punk that challenges me, the next guy who refuses to step in line. Hissing breath as I pound out combinations in the air, left-right, right-left, left-left-right.

There's always someone willing to play.

The Lincoln that's been following me since the Mass Ave bridge closes in, and instead of heading down Storrow through the Esplanade, I cut in toward Boylston and the Commons, hoping to lose him on the sidewalks.

Then safety in the North End.

I've been followed before. It's part of the job. There are rivalries within the organization, and pressure from guys trying to edge out the traditional family-style gangster shit. There are always guns on the loose, always targets floating around. Especially with the Blacks moving in on territory in Jamaica Plains and Dorchester. Blacks with guns cause all sorts of problems, especially as cocaine gets more and more popular.

For all I know, Alonzo fucked the wrong pimp's girlfriend, and there are mobsters with machine guns behind the darkened glass just waiting to cut me up.

For all I know, I've done something to piss off the Don, and the Lincoln is out to pin a pink slip on my body. Or the opposite: could be a war with Whitey and the Irish.

For all I know...

I sprint down alleys and up one-ways, hopping a fence to cross a block at one point. Nearly trip over two kids in a sandbox. The slap-slap of my shoes on pavement sounds desperate. A bum on the sidewalk holds out a hand but reconsiders. Cars zip past. Redlights glare like the eyes of enemies lurking around each intersection, trying to stop me long enough to take a bullet.

And then by Arlington, near the movie theater, the Lincoln squeals up next to the sidewalk and resumes pacing me. As if he knows where I'm heading. Not a good sign.

I slow until they pull up level, and stop. Panting.

The rear window rolls down to reveal a face creased with laughter.

"Paulie Gaeta, so glad we finally found you. Hop in, buddy."

"Fuck no. Who are you?"

He looks puzzled. "Why'd you stop then, if you weren't going to get in the car?"

"The way you follow. Very professional. If I were a target, you'd've done it by the river. Easy to roll the body in."

I lean over, hands on my knees, head hanging in exhaustion. Giving in to my winded feeling. Taking the opportunity to look between my legs. Scan my six. Then I stand and twist my torso to stretch out. And check for anybody I recognize—either friend or foe—on the periphery.

I'm on my own.

"There are better ways of disappearing a body than dumping it in the river. But that's not what we're talking for. Hop in. It's a chance to make some cash. Not a plot on your Important Life," he chuckled.

"I just started my run."

"No you didn't. We've been behind you for almost an hour. You're exhausted. Hop in."

"Don't really have a choice, huh?"

He smiles as he steps out and holds the door for me. A gold tooth flashes in his face, and he winks as he gets in after me.

"I'm Andrew Winston." He holds a hand out to shake, a meticulous hand wrapped in French cuffs and tailored navy wool. His graying hair lies slicked to the side and back over his ears, every strand in place. Including the little curl hanging roguishly over his forehead.

"I'm an associate of Mr. Bello—Don Aberto, rather. He told me you like to scrap." He speaks quietly, as if he never has to raise his voice, with a faint New England accent, like he'd suckled on chowder and cut his teeth on saddle leather, but moved on to international things.

"I don't know about that," I say quietly.

"Come on, kid, don't be so goddamn reticent. How old are you?"

I say nothing. The car features a stocked bar with an oddly shaped bottle labeled Louis XIII squatting beside a tall bottle of Stolichnaya vodka. The wood panelling looks genuine, and a small TV plays news on mute. The car smells like fresh leather and cigars, and suddenly I feel right at home. And relax into the seat.

"Look, I know you're twenty," he says, "and I can tell you like what you're seeing in here." He raps the window. "Bullet-proof glass. Twelve-cylinder engine. Steel-radial tires. Gas masks." He pauses to let that sink in. He offers me a Perrier, and I take down half of it. "I know how much you earn pushing buttons for the Don. How would you feel about making no less than three grand tonight?"

I can't help it. "That would feel pretty nice," I say.

"You bet it would. How's your stamina? How you feel right now?"

I drain the rest of the water. Feeling pretty great.

"How do you feel about fighting for money?"

"What, like boxing?"

"Sort of. But no gloves. Good-old-fashioned bare-knuckle fighting. One of man's oldest sports. Aside from running. And in this circle, you can even bet on yourself to win."

I once bet a Rolling Stones roadie twenty dollars I could knock him down before the next T-train came, but that was the most money I ever earned doing what I usually considered a training program for loan-collecting. Usually after scrapping, Alonzo and I would have to disappear and spend at least a couple weeks before showing face at the same bar.

"If you come with us tonight and fight, you get three grand no matter what happens. Just for showing up. Three thousand dollars, even if you get the tar beaten out of you."

"That would never happen."

"But if you win the fight, you get more. Five thousand. To win."

He explains that he hosts a monthly match in a Beacon Hill apartment he owns, and one of the fighters dropped out after bets had already been placed. Now that the guy is in no condition to fight anyone anymore, they need somebody to fill in the down side of the spread.

"The down side of the spread," I say.

"The spread's set. You're just a replacement—but a promising one, based on what I've heard, and I want to give you a chance."

Biology has given us two motives underlying every choice: Reproduction. Survival.

Everything else is in their service, and in turn, their one goal is to spread the species. First Me, and through Me, the common good. Every man for himself, and to the victor go the spoils—and the bragging rights. Fill your pockets and swell your chest. The American Dream.

If I get involved in this, it could launch me to the next thing. This isn't Cosa Nostra. This is Cosa *Mia*.

Or I could get my ass kicked, and crawl home with my tail between my legs or worse, possibly alienating the Don who'd backed me with his reputation. I'd have the three grand, but that's less than the value of my pride.

At Hanover, Winston tells the driver to stop before the light turns red.

To the right, the North End and the usual loan collecting and mobbing around with Alonzo. Same shit, different day.

To the left, a Beacon Hill brownstone, and something new, something fresh, something scary; possibly fatal, possibly golden. The opposing light flicks yellow.

"What'll it be, buddy? Left or right?"

There won't be a second offer. The car next to the Lincoln eases forward, anticipating the light.

Winston says nothing further, just looks at his fingernails.

The light changes. The Lincoln rolls forward.

"Left," I say. We head toward the Hill, in a direction I rarely go. A neighborhood of townhouses with gates and private security and yippy little dogs that you don't walk yourself.

The gold-domed State House glows in the early afternoon sun as we pass by. The trees along the sidewalks are bigger, more spread out. The parked cars are all BMWs and Benzes and Jaguars. The cobblestone streets are neat and level.

The Lincoln stops at an intersection.

"I have to put a blindfold on you," Winston says apologetically. Politicians live in this neighborhood. Politicians who may be at the fight. Politicians who don't want the constituents knowing their addresses. And rich people who don't want me coming back here on my own under any circumstances.

I'm here to entertain.

"No blindfold. Fuck that. I'll just get out here and walk."

"If you get out here, you'll be stopped by the security guard patrolling the end of the block, and when you don't have a good reason to be on this street, he'll either call the police or beat you with his nightstick. That guard has millions of dollars worth of attorneys and decades of political clout ready to back up any action he takes on behalf of the residents here." He pours himself a rocks glass of vodka and sips it. "Plus you'll be walking out on three grand or more. And that's just your *first* fight."

"When's the fight?"

"Quarter of seven. These men have work and families."

"You have cash on you?"

Disappointed, he frowns and shakes his head. "Don Bello had me under the impression you weren't just a cheap bruiser like that. He said you might be one to go far."

The fuck does he mean, cheap? A fight is something to get through and come out on top of. A fight is about who's better, who's allowed to continue, who's on top of the goddamn food chain.

And money is about money. If it's not there for the grabbing, it's not there. If I can't see it, it doesn't exist.

So fuck'im.

"Let me out. I'll take my chances." I put my hand on the door lever.

"Gaeta, look at me."

I look.

"You want to go on loan sharking and slinging dime-sacks for chump change your whole life? I'm telling you this right now and only once: this could be a shot for you to make a million bucks. But it only works if you have a little faith."

"Faith, huh? Well bless me, Father, for I have sinned," I tell him. "I haven't been listening to the numbers."

Winston smiles. "How long since your last full-body massage, my son?" He laughs at my blank look. "I don't want you to be all uptight if I'm putting hard-earned money down on you. How do you like Thai girls? I have one on staff. My in-house masseuse."

I shrug and take the black bandanna, tying it over my eyes.

ooooo

The front door clicks shut behind me. I yank off the bandanna and squint until my eyes get used to the orange parlor glow of lamps and a muted chandelier casting patterns on the hardwood and wallpaper.

The house is old, with thick moldings and framework. A broad carpeted staircase curves up into darkness, framed by gold-painted banisters. It seems impossibly huge inside. The maroon drapes in the sitting room match the stairs.

Two men in tuxedos sit in thick leather chairs smoking cigars and looking at us with the air of having been interrupted, until one recognizes and greets my companion.

Winston nods in reply and leads me down the long hall toward a drone of voices. He stops before a gold-painted door and grasps the knob.

"Here's your massage. Hungry? We'll feed you after you fight, if you're not too mashed up."

I must have frowned as he opened the door.

"Don't worry. You'll do fine. For now, enjoy yourself. Relax."

I walk in, and he closes the door behind me. A small woman wearing a kimono smiles and gestures toward a bed with a donut-shaped pillow at one end. I look around awkwardly until she takes my hand, leading me to the bed and peeling off my sweatshirt. She hands me a towel and turns away as I strip off my sweatpants and lie face down on the bed.

Then there's nothing but the grain of the wood floor underneath and the warm fabric of the bed and the girl's delicate fingers rubbing a scented oil into my back. There's no sound outside the slick *shh* of my muscles releasing years worth of tension. Limb by limb, inch by inch, fiber by fiber, my body relaxes under the girl's skilled touch, and I catch myself drooling slightly.

There's no telling what the next few hours will bring. I may wind up dead. Guys get killed in streetfights all the time, and even bar brawls usually end with two sirens, one screaming toward the hospital and one toward the drunk tank.

This is a submission fight. Winston's speech in the car echoes in my ears. In this fight the winner is the guy who is still standing at the end—however long that takes. You can tap out or go down and not come back up. No gloves. No wraps. Mouthguard required and provided—no one wants to have to clean up broken teeth. No shoes, no shirts. No timeout, no rounds, no bell.

Needless to say, Winston's reminder, *outside this room this fight has not happened.* No kicking, no biting, no low blows. Hit a guy while he's down, but only if he's still fighting. If you lose, you will never return, never speak to anyone present again.

And if I win?
We'll see.
Right.

There will be a referee to stop the fight when appropriate, and bandages, ice packs, and a physician for after the fight. And then plenty of booze and things to drown any pain once the excitement wears off.

Even a tough guy feels pain from time to time. *You'll learn to love it.*

I'm already learning to love this massage, the feel of a woman's hands moving slowly across my whole body, rubbing knots and stress out of places I didn't even know were tight until she suddenly makes them looser.

The same feeling comes over me, that tingling wave of feeling I get after the first few miles of running. The runner's high. The thing that makes roadwork possible day after day.

I can feel every piece of my body, all fitting together and gelling. I can feel the power in each of my fingers, the electricity running through my veins. I can feel the oxygen flowing to muscles, the commands transmitting from my brain.

I can see the fight.

I can see my opponent. Just ahead of me, glowering at me, unafraid.

I can feel my fists tighten into rocks. I can feel a thin smile spread across my face, splitting around a yellow mouthguard.

Before it happens I can see the first movement—a step forward and a hunching of the shoulders. He's throwing a punch.

So I duck before he throws, and throw my shoulder into his ribs just hard enough to distract him from my fist arcing under his arms toward his face.

Pop!

I see the life leave his eyes for an instant, and I back away to reload. Sweat and blood mingle and fuel the pressing noise of the crowd which is drowned out when a fist glances off the side of my head.

Deafening silence after the impact, until sound rushes back.

Before it happens I see myself jumping back to clear my head, hissing breath through the mouthguard and narrowing eyes.

Trying to see through the ringing in my ears, pep-talking myself to shake out the sparks in my vision, willing myself past the fear of getting hit again.

You'll learn to love it.

Calm, quiet on the massage table, I see myself lunging at this bare-chested man, aiming every jolt of anger, speed, power, force, control, love, hatred, instinct, feeling, behind the mass of my body. I see myself surprised at how easily his jaw gives under my fist. Taken aback at how stiff and fast he falls.

Before it happens I see him hit the floor.

I see him bounce.

Unsure what to do, I see myself waver, looking for guidance. He doesn't get up. A murmur passes through the crowd. The referee stands staring for a moment before dropping to his knees to watch for a tap-out or unconsciousness. Before it happens I see my opponent struggle to his knees and haul himself to his feet. Shaky. Cross-eyed. Angry. Dizzy and confused. Stunned. Swinging at the air.

Before it happens, I see myself look to Winston, who nods.

I see myself swing a brutal left hook, landing it perfectly between his temple and his ear, hear the *pop!*, feel the jar, smell the blood in his eyes.

This time he doesn't get up. The doctor feels his pulse, shines a light in his pupils.

I see myself turn away.

When it's time for the fight, Winston knocks on the door and tells the Thai masseuse to scram. Wearing sweatpants and no shirt or shoes, I walk with him out of the room and down the hall lit by electric wall sconces into what was once a library. A group of men standing around a rough semicircle of crowd-control-type fences, some smoking cigars, some nibbling at the remains of drinks, some not looking up when we enter. One even continues talking on a phone whose cord disappears around a corner.

One or two guys shake their heads distrustfully, disappointed that a replacement fighter has been brought in. These men who never hesitate to hire scab workers when the bottom line checks out, these men feel they're being cheated. These men who have no problem betting thousands on an illegal fight, these men bridle when their rules have been bent.

I make eye contact with the doctor in a white lab coat and nod. He nods back almost imperceptibly.

Winston escorts me into the makeshift ring, unhooks the connector, and slips in behind it to talk to me. He has a water bottle with him and an ice pack in a bucket.

Over the course of a minute or two the attention gathers on me. Guys in preppy suits, guys in power suits, guys in tuxedos, one or two leaning on canes—you'd almost expect to see the glint of a monocle held in place by a perpetually dubious look. Everybody looking. Everybody's evening entertainment in my hands.

I stand up straighter, feeling bigger, taller. I can feel the quiet power emanating from these Old Boys through the fluttering in my stomach, with here and there faces I recognize from TV.

I inhale the power as deeply and slowly as I can, concentrating on a rhythm.

My opponent appears down the hall.

With my breath I grow bigger. Bigger than six feet. Bigger than two hundred ten pounds. Bigger than my fists. Bigger than my skin. Bigger than my audible heartbeat. Every muscle tensed and hardened.

The attention in the room leaves me for a moment when the favored contender enters the ring. Then the eyes drift back my way, and I give them a show, standing calmly with my arms crossed, head thrown back in defiance of their sizing-up.

Fuck this guy. There's no reason to be afraid of him.

He walks up and shakes my hand hard. The freckles on his shoulders flash red with his pulse. A broad shamrock tattoo, ripped down the middle, crosses his chest. He outweighs me by a good thirty pounds and has longer arms. But long arms can be gotten inside of. These things you learn when you grow up street brawling. Get inside. Go nuts. Otherwise catch a haymaker and go down.

We both hold the shake too long, and the release is awkward. A handshake is many things. It's hello, goodbye, acknowledgement, agreement. It's a telling interaction, a meeting of spirits. To mess one up is a tiny tragedy shared by both participants.

We step back to our corners. And the fight begins.

ooooo

In the sullen turmoil after the fight, I find myself in an office with Winston. He leans on a huge redwood desk and watches a leafless tree sway in the courtyard.

"Helluva fight, kid."

"You say so."

He turns around. "Cigar?"

I shake my head.

"Whiskey?"

I nod.

"What kind?"

I stare at him. The hell you talking about, kind?

"Hmm. Try a scotch." He drifts toward a bar built into the wall and pulls out two short glasses. From a crystal bottle he pours an inch of a deep amber liquor into each, along with a few drops of water from a pitcher on the same tray.

"Try that," he says, thrusting a glass at me. "This will open your eyes to a whole new world of drinking."

I take it and sniff. Smells like smoky whiskey.

"Take a sip and let it hit your entire tongue—you really got no cuts? No loose teeth? Only that one bruise?"

I tilt the glass to my nose, letting the aroma bite clear my nostrils. Then a tiny sip. Smooth. Light. Honey. Fire. In that order and then back around, creating a circulation between nose and mouth that's uplifting and calming at the same time. After two more sips I pull back and look at the scotch through the lamp, tilting my head to see through my unswollen eye.

"This is a beautiful thing."

"Yeah," he says, "this is something you're going to like."

I've never signed a contract before. Not for my janitor job, not for the Don—fegittabadit. For too many obvious reasons.

But this before me is a short contract. One page long. Simple statements, rules, penalties.

It's not a legal document.

It's a polite way of indicating to the signee that *they're* aware that *he's* aware that he's signed up for a thing and there's no convenient way out until it's done.

A hundred fights.

A million dollars in just a few years. All cash. From there on, a few savvy investments buys a gold-plated retirement. Before I'm thirty. And then freedom. My own life, owing nothing to no one. Cosa Mia, free of debt, free of responsibility. Enjoying the ride after pounding the pavement to catch up.

An ostrich in the yard. I want an ostrich. And alligator-skin boots.

"Anything you want, you can have," Winston explains. "You just have to earn it. Ten thousand dollars at a time. Provided you win."

A hundred fights.

How many fights had I been in, in bars, neighborhoods, T stations, in yards, playgrounds, parking lots?

Enough to know I was pretty sure I didn't mind making money doing it. Especially six-figure money. Each year.

Up to now I barely knew what six-figures meant.

At the big fights I can still bet on myself to win, if I want. But any discovered bribery or cheating means a bullet in the heads of both guys.

"I imagine you're not the type to take a fall for cash."

"Pride is the only thing worth more than money," I tell him.

"Well said," he nods. "I hope you keep that attitude."

"The fuck's that supposed to mean?"

"Take it easy, kid. Don't take things so personal. You get over that, you might be suited to something bigger. A taste of real power. Political power. The power *behind* the power. So much bigger than your little fists."

I shake my head.

"The way you stand; the way you talk; the way you introduce yourself to a room. You like that surge of power, don't you?"

I do.

"I do."

"Well," he shrugs. "We'll see. That'll be a long time down. And only if you don't take too many punches. For tonight just enjoy the food."

"Fuckin' A," I say, and leave his office.

ooooo

It was Eliot's idea to set Holly up with guys he knew, for money. He'd done it before, he said, and even knew another girl who might be interested in management so she'd have a friend.

"It's great," he said. "You'll make more money than you know what to do with."

She did enjoy sex. And she did need money. Too many girls she knew worked long hours at restaurants where celebrities hung out, hoping to meet someone who'd carry them to stardom. When that didn't pan out, they just wound up jaded and crushed under the debt of languishing in LA on a part-time education track. That wasn't for her.

"You won't like everyone. But they'll still pay big bucks. Wouldn't you like to make thousands a week?"

She could save up and pay her way into business school. She could finish her GED and move on to something else. She could invest in the stock market and make millions. She'd given up on the veterinarian dream when she realized she'd have to put animals to sleep, but knew she had to figure something out when her boarding school refused to readmit her after she returned to the States.

"I'm telling you, I know so many guys! You could work a few hours a day and make six figures! I know what I'm doing."

They were sprawled on the bed in the apartment he'd rented for her, sweat drying in streaks, and a 45 whispering white noise from the dresser.

"I'm here to protect you, baby. I'll make sure nothing bad happens. Just follow a few simple rules."

No anal.

Condoms for everything.

Cash up front.

Only one nut per session, no matter how much time is left.

Work at home: out-calls are easy stings for the vice squad.

No pictures.

Keep some pepper spray Animal Repellant within reach—and know how to use it.

She started at $200 for a half hour; $360 for an hour. Eliot's "friends" were wealthy, he explained, and wanted only expensive things. High cost = high class in such people's eyes, even if they haven't seen the merchandise. She accumulated a dresser full of sex toys and costumes to satisfy any client's strange needs.

Holly eventually found herself shopping, seeing shows, going out for dinner and leaving exorbitant tips—as people tend to do who work in the service industry—and worrying less and less about the financial side of things.

The sex stuff was easy, and she earned so much money, putting a portion away every time, and blowing the rest on new bags and clothes and makeup and manicures and pedicures; she felt she was finally going somewhere.

The door would open.

Eliot would walk in, trailing a shy-looking "friend of his" client.

"Here she is," he'd say. "Even hotter than I told you, huh?" Then turning to Holly, "He knows the rate. He paid the cash." Then he'd flash the bills, sniff them, and stuff them into a cash box she kept on the counter, taking out his cut. "Do your thing, honey."

And do her thing she did.

It wasn't such a bad way to make a living, and who cared what Mama would think? It was *her* fault she was in this line of work anyway, taking her out of school like that in the middle of the semester. Plenty of great side benefits too—like tips and gifts, VIP parties and the trappings of the rich, plenty of free time and no set schedule.

It always took longer if the guy couldn't get it up. Too much trying. If it was up, it was in—and she was out sooner. But some old guys would pay top dollar just to wiggle it around for a while. And that made an hour go by even slower.

Her savings grew day by day, and every time she had to coax a flabby client with boner problems, she'd think about things like Eliot convincing her not to take Client 33 up on his offer of a porn-industry tryout. He was listed in her notebook as *Client 33: likes geek glasses and skirts. Wife. Divorced. No doggystyle. Likes nipple bites. Porn?* Or her growing fear of reprisal when clients like *Client 72: feather boa, lawyer girlfriend, blow, apartment in the financial district* invited her to take up residence as a long-term mistress with all the traditional benefits. Why should Eliot dictate her sense of responsibility? Why should he be the only thing standing between her and something better? Most of his clients were a bunch of nobodies with no influence beyond digits in bank accounts.

Their faces drifted out of her memory as easily as Mandarin words.

She'd always wanted to become a social worker. Help out more than just taking a handful of homeless guys out to lunch now and then, listening to their problems. With money and official credentials, she could help save the world.

She plotted out what she would do later, what movie she'd go see, what she'd have for dinner. She thought about waterfalls and leather jackets and sunglasses.

When the client finished, he'd pull out and tug off the condom, cleaning himself with the roll of paper towel she offered.

Then he'd leave.

The worst thing about the job was the overwhelmingly unsatisfying sexual experiences that left her horny all the time. She'd dip a menthol in a spot of cocaine left on the hand mirror in her nightstand drawer. Lighting it, she'd yank off the extra sheet she used to protect her eight-hundred-thread Egyptian cotton from clients, and lie back, toying with a new vibrator reserved for private use.

Then she'd count the spots in the ceiling panel and stub out the cigarette, drifting into sleep.

ooooo

My eyelids were drooping when Holly stopped talking and prodded my ribs. I perked up, sniffled, and stretched languorously.

"What time is it?"

"Who cares?"

We were off the clock. Curtains drawn; radio unplugged from when the alarm went off, scaring us half to death, and I yanked out the cord because I couldn't figure out how to switch the damn thing off.

Or no—she must have plugged it back in while I was dozing. The clock showed a few minutes after midnight. A song warbled from the little box with numbers.

Holly resumed her teasing stroke, tingling up my spine into a slight shiver. I could smell her on my skin, warm and alluring, with a briny sweetness that flared my nostrils and got my heart pounding southward once again.

She took my penis in her hand and leaned in to bite my chin. Her hair was still damp, and I shivered as it grazed my chest. I couldn't explain it, but I felt strange, like I'd missed a chunk of time, or a scene had been edited out. Maybe it was the blow. There was something missing—or something had been added, changed, manipulated.

Cut the crap.

Back here now. The present. Now. Just a trick of the light and the numbers flapping around in an enduring cycle.

The song drones on, something about *So long it's not true*. Sometimes I wish I listened to more music. Or paid attention more. For some reason, it just doesn't mesh with me. Maybe I beat on an off rhythm. Or maybe I'm some kind of musically retarded. I'm not even affected by commercial jingles. They just don't make sense.

Holly breathes words into the space between my thighs, prickling the hairs and exciting the senses. She smells like menthols and sweat, mingled with the floral or fruity lotion she put on after the bath. Her lips are hot against my skin.

I sigh, and stretch out, cradling my head in my hands. She kisses the taut skin, and rakes my hip with her nails.

"I've got a surprise for you," she murmurs, and wraps a robe belt around my wrists and through a wall-mount lamp over the bed, and ties a scarf around my eyes. Then she gets off the bed and shuts the bathroom door.

A soft knock at the door.

I ignore it, thinking it's Holly in the bathroom.

Knocking again, harder. The room door.

Shit. What, room service? Not a good time, buddy.

"I'll get it," Holly sighs, and I hear her tiptoe past the foot of the bed to the door. She twists the door handle, and gasps.

Then a *thud* and she screams, and the door bangs against its chain, and another *thud*, and the grate of screws wrenched out of drywall, and a clattering of chain gone slack.

Then   RRROOOAAAGGGGHHHHH!   and   I'm struggling against the knotted robe sash.

My hands are off the lamp. Holly screams and throws something which *pocks!* against the wall.

The bed lurches, and I roll off, twisting my wrists free of the sash. I dash toward the bathroom in darkness, reaching a thumb between silk scarf and forehead.

RRROOOAAAGGGGHHHHH!   and   I   hear   a sickening *plop!* like meat slapped on the table. His fist. He killed her.

But she bought me time.

I fling the blindfold toward the noise and sweaty reek, and lunge for the Walther on the bathroom counter.

Backlit by the door, the Tongan is just a huge shadow growing in my vision, lunging toward me, growling and slobbering.

The gun's tangled in the towel.

He reaches for me, and I get my hand around the grip, still wrapped in the towel, and wiggle a finger through the trigger guard.

Bang!

Bang!

Bang! Bang! Bang!Bang!Bang!

The gun stops firing, and I realize the slide is locked back. Empty. A tendril of smoke rises toward the checkered ceiling. The towel falls away, charred around two oblong holes. The Tongan lies prone, partially concealing a pool of blood spreading across the tile and soaking into the carpet.

Fucked.

Brrrrrring!

The phone.

Brrrrrring!

Holly lies half in the closet, legs sprawled under a soft robe.

Brrrrrring!

The room door hangs wide open. Anyone would have heard.

Brrrrrring!

It occurs to me to pull out the empty magazine and replace it

Brrrrrring!

with the other loaded one in my bag.

Brrrrrring!

What the fuck? Why is the phone ringing?

Brrr—

"Yeah?"

"Gaeta! Jesus, it's you." My promoter—booking agent—he sounds flustered over the tinny line.

"Yeah, why wouldn't it be?"

"I...I'm sorry, you're...you're probably with a woman. Listen, the guy you fought, that big Samoan guy—"

"Tongan."

"Yeah. He might've found out what hotel you're staying at..."

I counted five.

"What are you *saying*, Gary?"

"He...He might be after you. My secretary—she..."

I look at the blood-matted mane of hair, and see I shot the guy through the face and blew out the back of his head. I turn and locate five blood-spattered bullet holes in the wall.

"You have a secretary, Gary? That just seems fucking unnecessary—and *why* might this guy be after me?"

"Well, he's a sore loser. Apparently he's done this before. When he hasn't killed guys in the ring."

"Sore loser? Y'don't say! I dunno how sore he is now, though, Gary."

"Sounds like pretty bad. Someone said they saw him following you in a cab."

"Tell you what, Gary, you let me worry about the Tongan. I saw him earlier today. He won't be a problem. You just worry about my next fight, ok? Do your job. Maybe shoulda let me known about this lunatic yesterday, huh?"

"Yeah, sorry, Gaeta."

"Tell you what also, Gary. Get me a fight tomorrow or next day. I need the purse. And then I'm going to take off for a while. In fact, you probably should disappear too."

He answers with silence, spooked.

"What do you mean?"

"I mean, Gary, that your boy has already stopped by. You just missed him, matter of fact, you slimy little fucking crab—not to mention there's some collateral damage in my room here. And I'll tell you something else: this kinda feels like a setup."

"What? C'mon! You know how much money I make off you—alive and kicking ass. Besides—wait, what do you mean *stopped by*—Jesus! That room is in my *name*."

"Yeah, well, never mind that. You'd better get your ass somewhere I can meet you. This sore loser is cooling off in here as we speak, right next to a gorgeous young hooker connected to the ranch *and* those suits. You want to save your ass? Save mine first. Otherwise, I swear to God, I'll just take off and disappear, and then *you're* the one who's fucked."

ooooo

Still aglow in the victory of my very first bare-knuckle prize fight, I walked out of the steaming shower room into a waiting towel held by Winston's Thai masseuse who toweled me off more thoroughly than I would've thought reasonable.

Then she pointed to a suit hanging on a hook and left.

The suit was slightly too small, but it was nicer than any I'd ever worn before. And I had learned from Alonzo to dig nice threads. It was the color of midnight, made of the softest, thinnest wool. There was a tie that matched the pocket handkerchief, but I ditched it in favor of folding my shirt collar over the suit lapels with a few buttons open instead. The pants were close around my legs, flaring out slightly at the feet, an older style that I liked better than the awkward-looking shoulder pads and baggy slacks favored by my generation. I had my own shoulders and legs to show off: the tightness of the suit helped.

The shoes, though nice, didn't fit.

I stood in front of the mirror wiggling my toes for a while before deciding just to go eat the food that I'd seen and smelled after leaving Winston's office. Who notices feet anyway?

When I padded into the dining room, the first thing everyone looked at was my bare feet.

A model in a lycra dress sidled up to me with a full glass of champagne.

"Hey, you fought, right?"

I nodded and took her glass, draining half of it.

"You clean up good. Are you barefoot because you're training?"

I looked at her and said, "Yes. Yes I am."

"I've heard of that before. How does it help?"

"Um. Something about the toes...it's very scientific. Anyway, how about some shrimp?"

"Oh I don't eat meat," she said, holding up a long thin hand. "It makes you gain weight and turn boxy. No offense..."

"Bullshit," I said. "Shrimp isn't meat. And there's nothing you could ever say that would offend me. Grab me another champagne, willya?"

She drifted off, and I made my way over to the plate of cocktail shrimp.

"You don't want that shit, Gaeta." Winston took a shrimp out of my hand and put it on a plate held by his companion. "Shrimp is for suckers. Literally. Shrimp crawl around on the ocean floor eating all the leftover crap that drifts down. Have a porterhouse steak. That's more your style."

"Is that right?" I said, leaning over to grab the same shrimp. "No one ever pointed out to me my style before." I popped the thing in my mouth and bit it off at the tail, which I placed daintily on Winston's plate.

"Well. Your palate. Anyway, come meet somebody you're going to see a lot of in the next couple years."

The model approached with two champagne glasses and a broad red-lipped smile. I winked and waved her off as Winston led me away from the buffet and toward the foot of the dining table.

"Paulie Gaeta, this is Gary Duchenne. Gary, this is Paulie."

Gary stuck out a hand and smiled, tilting his head back slightly to look me in the eye. A well-trimmed vandyke drew the attention away from his thinning hair, which was long and wavy, sweeping around his ears as if holding on for dear life. Apart from the very top, it looked like a helmet.

His hand was small but firm, and I found myself liking him, even as he released the shake and sniffed through an aquiline nose.

"You like cocaine?"

I shrugged. "Never had it."

"It's the next Big Thing. The girls love it. C'mon, Andrew, let's go to your office and blow some."

"Gary."

"C'mon, it'll be fun. You gotta try this shit."

"Gary."

"It's no problem—I have enough for everyone."

"Gary, shut up. I'm introducing you to Gaeta for business."

"Yeah?"

Winston spread his hands in bewilderment. "Were you *here* thirty minutes ago? How fucking high are you? This is the fighter."

Gary's eyes went wide. Then he stuck his hand out again. "I'm sorry. I'm Gary Duchenne. Helluva fight. I didn't recognize you all dolled up like this. You clean up good."

"Don't mention it," I said. "The fight was pretty short."

"Gary's your contact for your fights."

"Agent extraordinaire," Gary corrected. "Let's hope they're *all* so quick. Nothing like earning thousands in a coupla minutes, am I right?"

"Nothing like it, Gary."

He stood up straighter, extracting himself from the pawing of a tall woman next to him. "Cigars?" he asked, reaching into an inner pocket.

"Let's talk in my office," Winston said.

He led us again down the hall toward his office, nodding and patting backs as he went.

"Paulie, I want to explain the structure of the next few years of your life."

Most of what Winston said for the next thirty minutes drifted right through my hearing, as I mostly thought about paying a visit to Francesca Battaglia and taking her for a ride on the motorcycle I planned to buy. That would for sure get me back into her good graces.

He talked about the death circuit that I'd joined as if it were some secret brotherhood, like an offshoot of the Freemasons who upheld the pure-violence end of the philosophy. Till death or quarter. The members were all guys with more money than they could burn, all guys who started on the wrong end of the law and never turned back, guys who simply had the law changed to keep themselves from feeling its wrath.

The bare-knuckle death circuit stemmed from ancient tradition. It predated any national boxing league by thousands of years, going back as far as human memory. An idea with no inception, no pinpoint beginning. A group of guys circled around two men with fists raised in defiance of each other's right to survive, goaded on by the crowd. Place the image in time: there is no limit to its scope; an idea for as long as there have been people interested in competition for its own sake, competition to pit top specimens against top specimens.

Over the course of human history, competition evolved into gladiatorial events evolved into wargames evolved into olympic games evolved into organized sport evolved into...whatever's next.

The human soul is so tied into the win that even people without the physical ability to dominate each other have a deep yearning to watch the brutal, carnal pitting of animal versus animal. And what animal is more vicious, more survival-hungry than the human?

These people, these suits who control the strings of society, who play the games of Fate, are willing to pay serious cash to watch a competition stripped of games, stripped of complicated layers, stripped of plotting and conniving and rhetoric, stripped down to its meaty, vicious essence. From their lofty positions—achieved not by muscle but by brains and metaphor, trickery and semantics, bullying, strategy, lies, manipulation—they look down to the sweaty trenches, longing to be involved in the thick of it.

Man on man. No padding between weapon and target. Nothing between bone and bone but a few layers of skin.

Basic, human, animal, raw competition.

My cup of tea.

There's two types of people in the world. The people who run the world, and the ones who think they're taking part. And both, whether they'll admit it or not, are attracted to the blood, sweat, and violence of making it through the next day.

You just have to dig through the cushions of luxury and the habits of comfort to find the animal sheltered within.

Like Francesca, with her long dark hair and smooth olive skin, is an animal—once you strip away the trappings of humanity, toss aside the fabric of propriety, expectations, demands, beauty products, and headbands that keep her contained. Lying back against a crowd of silk pillows in a splash of thick almost-black hair, lithe and frisky like a mink, alternating between squealing and shushing me, directing my hips with cool fingers, pressing against me and nodding when I do something right, pushing away and biting me hard when I don't.

Francesca Battaglia, who takes her time to teach me everything she wants me to know about sex; both of us learning learning learning, getting better and better—until it's so good we can't do it in secret anymore because we're both too loud, and even my landlady casts suspicious and disapproving glances at me whenever I drop off rent or collect my mail.

Francesca, who turned sex into more than just living masturbation, into an experience that wasn't preceded by a business transaction, who gave and took equally and freely and ruthlessly.

Francesca, whose hips and legs and breasts and lips became the reason to exercise my stamina and improve my flexibility.

Death or quarter, Winston was saying. Just like the old days. How much pain is your pride worth?

All of it. Any of it.

When I was little my mother left my father once for a few months. I don't know what happened between them, or why she felt the need to send him such a message. I don't care. When she came back, though, he welcomed her with open arms, apologizing and laying himself at her feet. From then on he was hers, acquiescing to her every whim, nodding and obeying her every order, sacrificing himself at her altar. He gave up. He bowed out. He capitulated.

I never forgave him for that.

But here was a chance to forget all that. A chance that tasted like the tobacco fields of Cuba and the peat fires of Scotland. A chance that felt like slender Asian fingers and creature comforts my parents never knew existed. A chance to pull myself by my own bootstraps into the next tier.

A chance at the American Dream.

There are many types of power in the world, and each depends on many others. As Winston hinted at the identities of some of the people who'd be betting on my future performances, I thought of Francesca tying my wrists to her bedposts and pouring Hershey's syrup all over my belly.

The day Francesca moved away to college out west, a part of me went with her that I would never get back. It left a hole that I filled with things like the hundred-fight contract; the smell of cash stacked by the inch; the sound of fifty spectators inhaling sharply with surprise when a fight ended so brutally, so abruptly; the taste of standing over my vanquished foe; the feeling of walking away having passed today's test, of earning a place in tomorrow's arena.

We who are about to die...

There are ways of getting out of your contract, Winston droned. But none of them pleasant.

I would have to get a new pad. My crap apartment might have been suitable for covert rendezvous with a girl like Francesca, who had other reasons to stick around than just the trappings of wealth. But it was not suitable for broads like that model Jeanine. I would need leather sofas, and a bar with crystal stemware, and artwork on the walls.

I'd need more suits. More shoes—alligator shoes. A motorcycle. A new leather jacket.

I'd need a good pair of sunglasses.

And a better gun.

Five thousand dollars in my pocket could make that happen.

Five thousand dollars was scratch next to what I was going to make, Winston promised. You're *in*, pal.

ooooo

"Your friend Alonzo, he's kind of a dumb."

I nod. Rosen hands me a steaming tea. He knows I prefer coffee. But he doesn't like how it makes his Brooklyn flat smell like burnt beans, he says. He sits down and folds his arms in the silk sleeves of a kimono.

"Dumb is dangerous in this game," he continues. "He knows when to shut his mouth?"

Most of the time. Even though he's older, the little punk listens to me because I'd have no problem beating him to his knees. Also because he knows I'm smarter. And handsomer. While I'm spending time and money with Rosen in New York for the sake of furthering our money-tree business, Alonzo's on the warpath with the rest of his wise-guy friends, trying to make his name in the latest street violence. Nowadays it doesn't take any kind of *omerta* honor to be a made guy. You just have to kill someone important to the other side. If Alonzo gets initiated, he's automatically *my* boss.

Criminal hierarchy means shit to me. I'm more interested in making money. And staying alive.

"Running cocaine is basically the same as running heroin," Rosen promises. "Just different clients. Senators and rockstars instead of beggars and painters. You make more money but you run more risks."

Marty Rosen knows the heroin game inside and out because he's been in its penalty box. He went to fucking Columbia for pre-law, he insists, before the spike caught up with him. He used to fuck Allen Ginsberg, he claims, until he got kicked out of school. Somehow he wound up in South Boston, with an eye on the streets and a needle in his arm. Half calculating queen, half slobbering slave. Never ever try heroin, he warns. The needle becomes a nail that holds you to the cross.

"Aren't you Jewish?"

"Yeah, of course," he says, getting up to flip the record. "So was Jesus. He was crucified. So was I. So I'm allowed to make the reference. There's not a day goes by I don't remember what it was like to wake up scratching at my collapsing veins, trying to relive the feeling of junk flowing to every dark corner of my being."

He's lucky to be out. He's lucky his business savvy and his rigorous upbringing allied to pull him out by the seat of his pants. He reminds me of this almost every time I see him. His Brooklyn mother would be proud.

The thing he doesn't like about the cocaine game is he doesn't like rich assholes who get all jittery and tweaky on coke, who are liable to get into fights over prices, or have overzealous bodyguards or shrill bitchy women in tow. He doesn't like cocaine because it's an upper and he's a downer type. He wants to chill. He prefers selling to people who will sit around on the nod, dangerous to nobody—as long as they have their spike.

I try to explain the shifting market but he holds up a hand.

"There will always be junkies. Control the supply; control the demand. Blow might be popular right now, but that'll change again too. It's just like the stock exchange."

Drug use undulates like fashion. In, out, retro, comeback, in, out, retro...history repeats itself. Everything cycles. Revolution just means one turn on a spinning wheel.

Before I went to New York to visit Rosen, it had taken me and Alonzo four weeks to cut, bag, and distribute our first two kilograms of cocaine, dealing only with people we knew and people they knew.

I told Alonzo, fuck this. We had to find people to sling for us. We needed employees. Wasn't worth it otherwise. The only problem was, we'd have to move bulk. And we had no idea how to do that.

But Rosen has been moving bricks of H for months. He doesn't tell me what weight, and I don't ask. But his apartment in the Village speaks volumes. A huge TV takes up most of one wall, facing a projector between two soft leather couches. I'm not into art, but I'd guess the paintings on the walls are genuine Someones. The whole ceiling in his bedroom is a big mirror, and the

blinds over his floor-to-ceiling windows are motorized.
He's a long way from when we first met him in Southie.
If there's anyone I trust to teach the game, it's him.

He refills my cup with tea. "The dangerous thing for
you will be getting too big too soon," he warns. "You're
ambitious. You're smart. You're not the type to watch
your feet as you're sprinting for the gold."

"Let me worry about that," I say, stirring the tea.

"I'm telling you. You pick up a lot of shadows on your
way to the sun. I've been getting a little freaked myself
lately. I might retire early."

"Retire? You're not even forty yet. You know how
much more cash you can make?"

"Do you know how much I have? I'd be set, kid, if I
hadn't taken it into my fool head that I need to buy an
island where they can never reach me. Now I got a
mortgage bigger than you can imagine. But I also own a
sovereign island. Private property."

"You're paranoid."

"That's how I stay alive."

ooooo

Not long after my introduction to the bare-knuckle
fighting circuit, Alonzo and I were running pretty major
weights of cocaine. After mucking around for a while
splitting keys into grams and eight-balls for street-
corner slinging, we stepped it up. With the help of
Rosen's connections. There was no point otherwise. The
bare streets were too dangerous. Because I put in most
of the investment capital, Alonzo was working for me.
He tried his hardest not to show he was sour.

"Hey, boss," he smiled. "What's shakin'?"

"Alonzo." I nodded. "Get me a coffee."

He stared at me. I stared back. Then I broke a grin. "I'm just fuckin' with you. I'm actually in the mood for scotch. Go get me a Johnnie Red."

We went to one of our bars, and I sat down while Alonzo fetched the drinks. He came back with a girl he knew.

"Alonzo, what the fuck? This is a business meeting."

"But we're in a bar."

"Lose her, Alonzo, we have shit to do. Get her number and call her later. Jesus."

"Hey, man," he said, when he got rid of the girl. "How come you never want babes?"

"That's the stupidest thing I ever heard. You just don't know *when* to do *what*. You piece of shit. That's why you'll never make it up the ladder."

He made as if to tussle like we used to, but stopped when he saw the shadow of a gun on my hip under my suit coat and remembered his place. I had long ago ditched the .22 for a custom-grip Colt Python .357 Magnum, mainly because it was a huge piece that would scare the shit out of any adversary so I wouldn't have to use it. But after shooting a few boxes of rounds through it, I liked it for the weight distribution, the heft, the oneness with my hand, the mule kick. Ever notice how powerful it feels to hold a balanced gun? Try it. *Tell* me there's not a heady rush. Chest swells. Hands flex. Jaw clenches.

"Come on. We have work to do." I slugged the rest of the whiskey and slid out of the booth.

Six months later Alonzo was killed in the toilet at his cousin's club.

He'd been making deals on the side, adding some of his own cash to our purchase orders to buy a few more keys each time, which he cooked into crack rocks and distributed to black dealers in Southie.

Somewhere along the line he stiffed some asshole nobody curb-sucking hood who was able to find out where Alonzo hung out on which days. I was always telling him not to be so predictable. They followed him into the restroom and sprayed him ragged with a pair of Mac-10s. His blood clogged the restroom drain.

Francesca refused to talk to me at the funeral.

ooooo

Do you ever have the feeling that you've woken up into yet another dream? Like you're not really where you think you are, and not who you expect? Do you ever lose track of time, lose track of vision, lose track of sensation? Like everything's a jumble but then you realize there's nothing around?

You're falling.

You think you're falling. But there's no visible movement. Just a feeling of gravity going the wrong way, everything rising, skin prickling, air ripped from straining lungs...

I was elbow deep in a gym bag full of cocaine when someone knocked at the door. The gym had been closed for four hours, and anyone who would know what was going on was already inside, helping stuff bags.

Boom boom boom.

A very official-sounding knock. Herald of doom.

"Get the guns," I said.

Like a spec-ops squad, we crept into the dim hall near the reception desk with shotguns and SMGs. Outside, summer darkness sat heavy over Boston. The plate-glass facade was empty.

"Check the back," I said. The security screens by the sign-in forms showed nothing. A chill snaked up my spine.

Then the back store-room door blew out.

A concussion grenade leveled my crew.

"GAETA," a megaphone barked, "COME OUT, HANDS IN THE AIR. THE GYM IS SURROUNDED."

I racked my piece. There was no way they were getting me alive. Hefting a key of coke, I slit the bag and flung it up through the doorway at the SWAT.

Another flashbang through the cloud of cocaine dust.

Ears ringing, I leaned around the jamb and fired into the powdery smokescreen. My guys were all hog-tied with flex-cuffs, but I aimed low regardless, and sprayed bursts toward the corners of the room hoping to catch the cops.

Tears poured from my eyes, and I started coughing, choking. My throat closed, nose burning, skin crawling. They were poisoning me.

A gas-masked stormtrooper loomed out of the smoke and punched me on the side of the head, surprisingly weakly, but I went down anyway. Knee jammed into my back, he wrenched my wrists into cuffs and yanked me to my feet.

"You have the right to remain silent," he said, arm crooked around my elbow and spring cosh stuck between my legs. He finished the Mirandas as he pulled me outside and down an alley toward the waiting paddy wagon.

"Oh Paulie," he crooned, "you're so fuckin' fucked."

"Don't call me that. You call me Mr. Gaeta, you cop prick."

"I don't need to call you anything, pal. No one's ever gonna *see* you again."

"Don't count on it, buddy."

"Oh yeah? Friends in high places?"

"Something like that."

He closed the van door and I sat in sour silence for what felt like hours before we rumbled off toward an interminable stretch in and out of court, while I enjoyed the county's orange-clad hospitality

The one thing worse than the handcuffs and ankle shackles was the pair of shining brown eyes watching from a toddler's height on the hard wooden benches of the courtroom. A room full of ghosts, a haunting few gathered to mourn a damnation. The weight of the thing never quite settled, never quite understood. Not even on that awful day when you realize Dante's not coming back, and his last visit was the last. Whether mastered by his mother's pushy whispers, or frightened by his father's chthonic digs, the boy has decided to take another course of life. And you can't blame him, really, for leaving this stony hell behind.

ooooo

Someone passes on the catwalk outside Rosen's cell. He glances over despite himself. "There's no way you can beat this young guy," Rosen says. "You're fucked. You're not in your prime and you've been wasting away in a cell for years."

"That's not quite how I was thinking."

Marty Rosen runs a hand over his cropped grey hair and stares at the pawns for a while. Then he takes a bishop with his king-side knight. "And now you fucking got *me* involved in your little squabble. Just because you didn't have the heart to say no."

Just because you didn't have the heart to say no. Is that what happened? Have you lost your toughness, big guy? Has the great Paul Gaeta gone soft?

"Look c'mon, I was startled."

"Startled into making a deal that would only fuck both of us? You really think this kid has enough sway to bring the brothers down on you? You really think he matters to you, or that I really need his ass?"

With his influence, he pretty much has first right of refusal on any of the girlie boys. As the main inflow valve, he's valuable enough to all the petty junk slingers and the H-sucking plunger boys that he enjoys a reasonable protection. With Rosie out of business, the joint would experience a hell of a dry spell, which would result in fidgety wars in every corner of the yard. Marty knows this. The inmates know this. The screws know this.

"Startled because I was thinking about my boy. Haven't heard from him in a long time. *Check.* And I don't know much about this kid, except he's a talker. And brave. He came to my door and literally showed me his asshole."

He frowns briefly and looks for a piece to block the check. "So what happens if you lose your big gladiator fight to this guy, and everyone knows I'm your friend? What happens when I'm balls-deep in this kid, and one of the Delany Brothers happens to walk by just as I'm exhibiting the full joy of complete ownership all over his face?"

"That's *your* problem. You own him, gift ribbon and all."

"The gift that keeps on giving. Some fucking gift." Then he grins. "He is pretty fresh, huh?"

"Come on, you queer. Your move."

He ponders the board with his classical style—which means he takes approximately five centuries to make a move—and blocks the check with a queen-backed pawn.

"I'm not gonna lose."

"Have you seen that guy Big J? I mean, be serious."

"What are we talking about here, Marty?" A pointed wave at the chessboard. "Head in the game, buddy. When we're playing chess, we're playing chess—not solving the world. I'm just looking at all the angles."

He looks up. Looks down at the other bishop. Frowns. Looks up.

"Then maybe you see something I don't, pal, because from where I sit," he moves his queen to take the bishop, "checkmate."

A short silence.

"Look, Paulie, I've been with you—almost from the start. We've been pals—how long? I'm telling you: find another way out."

"Marty," a low growl, standing and raising a hand as if to sweep the hand-carved soapstone pieces off the board. "I'm telling *you*: don't worry about it. He's going down. Can you just provide some moral support? And maybe come along...just in case?"

"Go fuck yourself, I should say. It's impossible, I should tell you. But—and this is a big juicy Latino butt—there's a lot of dope money behind this guy

Robinson. Even if he can't come through with the Delany guys. I'll take his connection and roll over it in two years."

"I see."

"As long as nothing goes wrong..."

He ruminates in silence, collecting the chess pieces and putting them back in their shoebox. Then he looks up. "I'll come see you fight. If only to call the coroner afterwards."

"I tell you what, you pompous little fuck. Why don't you lay a wager on that guy. Then we'll see who finds what funny."

It's funny how the very fact of limiting something creates its value. When there's no cash money allowed in prison, inmates find a different kind of currency. Whatever's in limited but regular supply. Marty takes the offered postage stamps, which you can be sure he won't lay on some black galoot.

"I don't find this funny at all. You've bitten off more than you can chew. This fucking schwartza is the size of Shaquille O'Neil. And you are old enough to be his poor father."

"Look who's talking, gramps."

"Yeah, well I may be older than you, but I'm going to live longer, clearly. You dumb wop."

"How can you sit here telling me what's age-appropriate when you're still glowing from your most recent encounter with your newest boy-toy?"

"My new catamite has nothing to do with age, nor violence. He cleans and does things for me, and in exchange, I grant him the warmth of my seed."

"Aw you're fucking disgusting, you know that?"

"That's how I've stayed out of trouble for so long."

"You mean 'cause you suck off the warden every coupla days?"

"No, he wouldn't go for that. He's more interested in the clinical-grade H I bring in for him. Uncut. He's a purist."

"You know, I always *was* sort of curious how you keep your business alive from Inside."

Part of paying your debt to society means the few pennies you make in the laundry or the commissary or the kitchen go directly to the government coffers. Which means it gets misplaced and misspent. Or launched off the wing of an F-15 in some sandy hell. The only sure thing is, it doesn't wind up in your bank account.

Every inmate knows he's just fodder for big business. That's why some guys refuse to work at all. Housing an average federal inmate costs about the same as the median annual wage in this country—and it's a guarantee the license-plate manufacturers and the school-desk assembly companies and whoever else employs convict slave labor don't foot that bill. The taxpayers do.

Marty's business proceeds are in the hands of someone he trusts—or pays—on the Outside, being funneled into an island he owns under a different set of papers, somewhere off the Caribbean coast of Colombia, near Cartagena. The guy's a fucking genius.

"If I went around telling people, I'd never have kept my business. So mind your own."

"Alright alright, old man. You know I'm just teasing you. So, same time tomorrow?"

"Why don't I just save us both the trouble? Checkmate."

"Very funny."

Time for count. Due to the usual snafus—like general lockdown after two big groups of guys went at each other with broom handles and squirts of acetone in the yard, or routine inspections with the governor—it's two or three days until the next brotherly chess game.

ooooo

She wakes up with her face in the carpet, with her face in the short-shag multicolored flooring, with her face in the horizontal hideaway of countless spills, unimaginable filth, and innumerable stories, most of which she knows already.

She wakes up and immediately wishes she hadn't, streaming tears burning down a throbbing face, pain radiating down her neck, up her temples, across her crown, and echoing in her ears with a fast staccato heartbeat.

She wakes up and can't see through one eye, throwing depth perception out the window and rendering everything flat and meaningless. It takes a while of blinking, a length of groaning, and an instant of recognition to realize there's a body—an enormous body—lying like a mountain just out of her reach sprawled next to the bathroom; a mass, topped by a matted puff of hair and wallowing in a big circle of scarlet.

She wakes up and this feeling she has is like when she told Eliot she no longer needed management, announced with finality that she no longer had use of his services.

You're fucking kidding me, Eliot had screamed then. *Where would you be without me?* He flung a chair across the room, kicking at the pieces after it splintered against the wall. *The fucking street, that's where, you dumb slut.* His eyes blazed like an angry rooster, and he slapped her full in the face.

That time, when she'd woken up, *she* was the one covered in blood. The slash across her palm took fourteen stitches, and never healed quite properly. Even pissed as he had been, Eliot couldn't bring himself to slash her face or her tits. Her time then was worth $300 for a half hour and $550 for an hour, the same price to spread her legs as to sit and listen to your problems—and Eliot would never destroy that ATM, never squander his access to what she had to offer.

She pushes herself slowly, excruciatingly to a sitting position, leaning back against the cockeyed closet door, trying to calm her racing heart and fighting the nausea that swells with the pain. Then she throws up, watching the bile seep into the carpet.

The fighter. The sex. The hot tub. The coke. The cock. The door. The monster. The shock. The blackness.

A small handgun on the bed. A few shells on the floor. A charred towel. Blood spattered on the wallpaper.

She was alone that time when Eliot had slashed her hand. Somehow she dragged herself to the phone on the nightstand, rummaged through the drawer for a phonebook, found the Gideon Bible instead, and dialed 9-1-1, expecting Jesus to answer the phone.

This is Holly, she'd whispered.

What's the emergency?

My hand. Blood. Eliot.

Did you cut yourself?
Eliot. I think cut me, Eliot.
Where are you, Miss?
My room. In. Um...Marriott.
Can you elevate your hand?
Like, lift it?
Yes, please try to raise your cut hand over your head.
Her vision swam.
Her heart leapt in her throat. She gagged.
What's your name, Miss?
Holly.
Do you know what room number you are in?
Same as always. Room. Eight-thirteen. My birthday.
An emergency crew will be right there. Can you sit tight and tell me what happened, Holly?
What happened.
Eliot had snapped. There was nothing he longed for so much as control, and she'd taken that away, preferring independence, even if it meant fewer new clients and a less-organized schedule. Holly didn't need anyone to look out for her, to provide sources. For that extra ten percent, she could do her own client seduction and maintenance. Forget Eliot. The fucking prick. Little chickenshit Napoleon, strutting around with his rooster's attitude and chipmunk's stature. She could go into clubs and pick up new clients on her own. She didn't need to keep someone around who would hurt her.
And now here she is again on the floor, with a throbbing jaw and a hazy recollection of how she wound up here. Her hand, permanently half-curled from a

tightening of the scar during healing, is bright purple with the pulse darting through, and her vagina feels tender and stretched. But then, she remembers where *that* came from.

But the body. What about the body? She is suddenly awash in fear, fear that he's dead, fear that he's still alive, fear of how he was killed, fear she'll be suspected, fear that maybe she did kill him and couldn't remember, fear of something vague. The room door is closed tight, the lights still off.

Holly rolls herself onto her knees, slowly transferring weight to her toes, and gently pushes herself to standing. The room tilts, wavers, finally levels out. The left side of her face feels like the hot, used side of a pillow in summer. Her mouth tastes coppery. She probes two loose teeth with her tongue, and tears roll silently down her cheeks.

Her purse is on the counter where she left it. The fighter's suit coat and shoes are gone. The emptied bottle of rosé champagne lies on its side on the nightstand, like a drunken sailor given up.

Back then, the first thing Eliot had sent her by way of apology was a dozen roses and a bottle of Dom Perignon. He had it sent to her place by special delivery, and then showed up as she was paying the delivery boy that Eliot had neglected to tip.

She raised an eyebrow, sniffed disdainfully at the roses, and tossed them on the driveway before retreating inside to enjoy the bubbly on her own in the bathtub.

Eliot alternated between knocking and ringing her doorbell every five minutes for three hours before he finally left her in peace, long after the water had gone cold and she'd hopped into bed. Alone.

A couple months later Eliot walked into a café where she'd been having a coffee, asked her how everything was going and took a seat before she could tell him to fuck off.

He asked about business. He asked about clientele. He asked about money and happiness and loneliness. He mentioned knowing lots of new rich guys he'd met at his new country club, rich guys with fat wallets and skinny cocks, with only a few hard-ons left in life, for which they'd pay big bucks for proper treatment.

She smiled and touched his hand and leaned toward him when she said calmly, *Eliot, you're really sweet, trying to help me out like this, but quite honestly you're taking up a lot of my time that I could spend making money from creeps like you instead of talking to them for free. I have my own clients now, and they're better than anyone you know.*

He reared back as if to slap her, but decided otherwise when she clinked a can of pepper spray on the table and smiled sweetly. He stood up to leave, turning at the last moment to throw a five on the table for her drink.

The next time she saw him, nearly three weeks later, he gave her $1,000 and looked at his watch.

How long, he asked, licking his lips.

Half an hour.

You must be doing well.

She nodded. *That's gratuity not-included,* she added.

Though she rarely took house calls, she let him in, and guided him to the bedroom. He immediately unbuttoned his shirt.

Let's make this quick, he said. *I have a lot to discuss with you.*

A red light on the bedside phone blinks patiently. She ignores it and reaches instead for the Gideon Bible in the drawer. As she picks up the telephone, she flips at random through the book.

Emergency Dispatcher. What's your emergency?

ooooo

The funny thing about chess is that the king is never killed. Winning a chess game means forcing surrender. Maneuvering the pieces; action and reaction, strategy and counterstrategy, until there is no next move. A situation called zugzwang, on the last page of this old dictionary by the toilet. There is nothing the opponent can do but end the game. Beg quarter.

"I know how I'm going to win." Words of bravado, sitting down at the chess board across from Marty. A double row of white figures lined up for battle. A checkered field of No Man's Land. Why did he give himself the black pieces this time? Why does he want the second turn?

When you've played chess nearly every day for the last eternity, the hand-made pieces take on lives of their own. The bishop with the chipped miter—the result of a tantrum long ago. The black queen slightly taller, slightly more imposing than her white counterpart. The carefully carved kings with the lithe and supple bodies that Marty goes for.

The pawns lean down to tighten their greaves. A knight tests his blade against a leather gauntlet. The white queen sniffs indifferently at a nosegay.

"The only way you can win," Marty chuckles, "is to cheat."

"How do you know I'm not gonna?"

"Well I don't. But you can't really cheat in chess unless I look away and you move pieces around."

"Check."

"Very funny." He matches the classic double-space pawn advance.

He sits on the edge of his narrow mattress—queen-size, he calls it—and props his chin on a fist. You can tell he knows his reversal of the typical black/white roles has done its trick and spread seeds of doubt.

"Your move, hotshot."

In this game, the loser from the previous game has to kneel or squat. The coveted bed-edge seat is only for the winners. Marty Rosen is not a man who likes to give up his place on the bed. This is a high-stakes game, and he usually wins.

If you stand, you can see the whole board, bird's-eye-view, which has its benefits. Patterns emerge. Mathematical schemes and lines, linking with, crossing over, skipping on to other squares, but always dictated by the battlefield grid. It's like a squadron of fighters with no personal radar, no radio, just a perfect view of the map version of the battle. Except, then you get tired, you get antsy, you get in a hurry.

If you kneel or squat, you're at the level of the pieces, slogging through the trenches with the boys in uniform. This is useful too. You get a gut perspective, an intuitive level of understanding. You get the feeling of the game, and at that point, the game disappears, and it's a thing of survival. Except, then you're on the defensive, then you're reacting, and then you lose.

Rosen knows this. He knows this intimately, to the point where if you ever tried to describe it to him, he'd scoff at your inadequate philosophical language. Marty Rosen likes to say only two types of people can be good at chess—and this from a guy who won national titles before he got involved with nips of morphine early in college to help him cope with nerves. He likes to say only politicians and cons can be good at chess. He likes to say he didn't even start learning the game until after he lost his last rook to the system; until he was locked in the castle.

Half the time he's full of shit and just likes to hear himself speak, but it's part of the game to listen and absorb. It's part of the game to connect it to all layers of life. It's part of the game to ascribe importance to anything. Without that, there's just a grid of black and white squares, a few spindly sculptures, and two bored animals. The only real importance there is to the game is that you've decided to play it. Marty knows this. Paulie knows this.

And that's why no one pipes up and says why not just sit on the toilet facing the bed. It's all about what's at stake.

But when you're trying to see the whole board, trying to preserve the angle looking at the lives of the pieces while at the same time maintaining an eye in the sky, the grand scheme is illuminated. There are disadvantages though, to every position. Sitting on the bed is comfortable, and comfort can lead to blunders.

But you know how to win. A strategy has been decided upon. A move. A series of moves. The only way to topple Goliath.

"I'll bet you a lot on your secret island when I get out. If you still remember me."

"You're shitting me."

No.

"You don't know where my island is. And anyway, you'll be leaving long before me, and in no condition to be taking islands from people. More like in a body bag."

"I'll win."

"You won't."

The first move is the hardest. What strategy to employ? The very act of initiating it sends a scatter of calculations and counterstrategies out the window. Like on a chalk board in the prison classroom, where you've written equations and proofs and matrices, erasing parts here and there, adding, subtracting, dividing, hiding. And don't forget the imaginary numbers. The things that can't exist, but do anyway because they've been thought of by some nerd.

The system is ready.

And then you find out what the x-value is, and suddenly every line, every number is suspect, and the eraser comes out and dances around the chalk, and lines appear and reappear, and moves play out in ghostly fantasy, and you try try try to puzzle out what the other guy is thinking.

What does it mean that you've chosen to squat, when you usually stand? What is going through Marty Rosen's head as he lifts a resolute hand and pinches his knight by the mane, moving it two squares up and one across?

"So you get a piece of my island, huh? That's how you want to play this?"

That's right. That's how this gets played. A solemn nod.

"What if you don't win? What do I get?"

"The North End."

He raises an eyebrow, intrigued if skeptical. There hasn't been a Friday night gone by when he hasn't pleaded with Adonai to open the heart of Paulie Gaeta so that he might be magnanimous enough to share his connections to the guys in Boston who run the fuel injectors pumping heroin into the crooked cobbled streets of that thirsty city.

"Bullshit."

"Scout's honor." Three fingers held up in the classic sign. And a firm handshake. Then a pawn moves up two spaces. Marty stares at it, teething the inside of his lower lip. It takes ages to become familiar enough with a person to know his or her giveaway cues. The idea of tells—and how everybody's got one—is much older than the game of poker.

But more important is being able to see several moves ahead. The player who looks deep enough into the myriad possibilities is the one who makes the right moves, the one who guides the other pieces down the right path—which leads to obliteration or victory. It's only a question of how far Marty is seeing.

The next few moves are a blur. There's only one opening. The rest is just fluff. Pawns forge forward and pawns die, trampled under the hooves of knights, or trod down by the burnished leather of the bishops' boots, and all the while blindly moving toward certain slaughter at the behest of their king and queen, who in turn are controlled by divine rules and whim.

Patterns emerge.

Marty is playing cautious. Intending to throw his opponent off guard, he's become unbalanced himself. If deception exists for *me*, he's thinking, it can exist as a tool for anyone. Introduce doubt, and it spreads like mustard gas both ways across No Man's Land.

During a high-stakes game of chess, players' heart rates approach levels experienced by Olympians during the final heat.

But this is an unusual case. Because of cheating.

Or rather—expanding the game without first informing the opponent. The oldest trick in the book. *His* heart is racing: he wants Boston.

There's something so comforting about exclusive knowledge. Esoteric awareness. Like the girl who yearns for the man who seems to have a secret, who yearns to get in on the enigma. The secret. The truth. The why. The answer to the unknown question.

A knight stumbles into the teeth of Rosie's queen. A rook sidles out from behind its pawn. His queen-side castle. The last bishop sliding to the flank. Pawn down. Pawn down. Pawn down. Check. He's trying to frighten. An unbacked attack. Foolish. A rook comes to block and threaten. He retreats. A pawn falls. His queen threatens. Rook backs bishop. Bishop attacks. Check. Backed up but not complete. His state of mind must be just where it's most vulnerable. You can almost hear the thudthud, thudthud, thudthud coming from his stenciled sweatshirt. You can almost taste his concentration.

The deeper he thinks, the less he'll see of the scheme. He's hunched over on the bed, wrinkled eyes level with the heads of his pieces. This smart man, this chess player, this nutcase who turned himself in and got himself locked up when his streets got too hot and he began to fear them; who used the system as a hotel or safehouse from where he could keep directing the heroin game outside the range of junkie habits and junkie weapons and junkie misery, controlling the strings away from the temptation of his own supply, which still whispered his name sweetly every time he saw it. This smart man who, in a few years when he gets out, will be pushing retirement age, enjoying 500-style Fortune, all tax-free and tidy, hidden from the most scrupulous of g-man nitpickers. He's worked for his keep. Just like all the poor saps in the American Dream at their desks in their ties with their pocket calendars counting down til the next vacation—only he doesn't punch out at the beginning and end of each day. His work week is measured in years.

But right now he's just a little balding pawn, and the only possible way to ruin this would be to tell him so.

A premature check can tip your hand, exposing your entire gameplan to the enemy, like when Bill Belichick a couple years ago got caught taking unauthorized video footage to prepare for Sunday. Can you blame the guy? His team was tits! Every Pats game they put on in the common room has been an utter joy to watch, like a chess game with real players; like a bare-knuckle fight on a macro scale. He had to keep it going somehow.

Check.

Marty backs away from the white queen, and the bishop slides over to join her. He suddenly realizes she's been left exposed to attack from his knight, and he bites. Crucial mistake. Without a queen there's almost no way to defeat a skilled player without luck and guile.

A few more moves, and the game's over.

"Checkmate," he announces. There's no glee in his voice. The game felt dirty, somehow tainted. Like he knew it was the last game, and it turned out not to be a polished classical experience, but a harsh foray into the Devil's own music, the rasping, reeling beat of jazz. The only jams worth listening to.

"Great," a genuine smile. "Same time tomorrow, then?"

He looks up with empty eyes and a hollow look about his mouth.

"What?"

"Do you want to play again tomorrow or what?"

"But you're..."

"I'm what?"

Then he perks an ear, like a dog hearing an inaudible whistle. His eyes glint, and he grows a grin, the dawning of realization that he just won the prize. "So—who's your guy in the North End?"

"Whoa whoa, buddy, don't get ahead of yourself."

"I won."

"So?"

"So you said if I won, you'd give me your Boston connect." He stands up, aggravated. "Aw c'mon, man, don't tell me you're fucking reneging." He dashes the pieces across the cell into his concrete corner. "That's pretty fucking low, man. We're friends here."

"What you said was—and correct me if I'm wrong—that if *I didn't win* you'd get my guy in the North End."

"Yeah."

"Only I was talking about the fight tomorrow. Me against the black mountain. I told you I know how I'm going to win. Isn't that what we were talking about before?"

He stands there blinking, a fresh realization dawning.

"You mean to tell me you were bullshitting me the whole time?"

"Yeah. Listen, you're still so sure I'm losing that fight, so what's the big deal? I die; you keep your whole island."

"No no no, if you *lose* I keep my island. You don't have to die to get out of that one." Brows knit, he takes the offered envelope.

"This is an introductory letter to my guy. To be opened if I buy the farm. I'm a man of my word."

"You fucking prick. This whole time I thought you were just nuts, playing one chess game for such a big stake."

"That's the game, buddy. It is what I say it is. Checkmate."

ooooo

It's easier to imagine Holly getting up and walking away. Why not? She's a tough little bird. She's been hit before, hurt before. She survived. That big fucking galumph—shoulda shot him in the restaurant; shoulda killed him in the ring. Shoulda, coulda, woulda: the constant retrospective nightmare.

Sometimes, when you don't really know something, you might as well imagine it better than it could ever be.

Holly getting up, making that 911 call, walking out on her own with just a throbbing headache and sore jaw.

Picture heaven. Why bother with hell? Especially if you're already pencilled into somebody's version of it anyway.

Holly hangs up on the emergency dispatcher and finds her purse. The haze begins to clear as she closes the door and walks down the hall. There's nothing to connect her here. No fingerprints on file, no priors or reasons for her to be around. No witnesses that would remember anything. No paper trail.

The benefits of working for cash.

From here she can disappear. She can retire. Move. Start over. She can abandon all her loyal clients and set up shop somewhere else. Or go back to school. Her possibilities are endless.

She's supposed to have another appointment next week for the guys at the ranch, some sort of bachelor party, but they have no way of finding her if she leaves. A clean slate. A true chance to start over. How often does anyone get such a chance? More seldom than anyone might dream.

But for Holly, the world is not a laid-out series of strategies. For Holly, the world is what she makes it, a product of whatever action she chooses in a given moment. For Holly, the world grants plenty of start-over possibilities. For Holly, this throbbing pain is just the ache of rebirth.

Her scars run deep, as one would expect when the pain inside comes to the surface to be released in blood. It's comforting over time to watch each self-inflicted cut scab over, tighten, fade. A reminder of healing. Each scar a story. For each story a scar.

She's done it before.

She'll do it again.

A failed marriage; threats on her life by a frightened politician; losing her bank to a pyramid scheme—none of that bullshit will ever keep her down. Any failure results in a chance to start over. A chance to heal.

At times she'll sit by the koi pond and contemplate the tectonic shifts that molded her life as it is—whatever brought her to this interchangeable moment. She'll finger whatever sleek garment she has on, and smile a small private smile that any man would sell his soul to understand.

She'll enjoy the smile to its completion, and round it off with a deep sigh, trailing her fingers in the water and closing her eyes against the bright sunlight.

ooooo

Accumulate enough Good Time, and you get little privileges like extra paper and felt-tipped markers, or better lunch slots, or more pay at your job—maybe bring you from $0.86/hr to a full dollar, after taxes. You can feel a sense of accomplishment, assured that you're well on your way to rehabilitation, and that you're no longer a danger to society to be kept out of the way. You can feel that you're making progress in the system, adjusting your behaviors to fit the mode.

And you can trade in a piece of collateral like a CD player or diary or a pair of hand-carved chess queens so you can play the musical instruments in the equipment room at the back of the Commissary.

Anyone with stellar behavior can play them an hour at a time. Other inmates can gather to listen or play along if they choose, but it's the only common area you can play in, unless it's arranged beforehand as something official and available to all, like a talent show or whatever. This keeps fighting to a minimum when someone tough plays terribly. *Some* of their rules make perfect sense.

No one in the Commissary notices if you've ever played their piano. No one points out that you've never shown any interest in any musical instruments before. No one guesses at your reasons for the sudden need to plink out a harmony. No one in the Commissary notices or points out or guesses much of anything, on purpose.

Commissary clerk is one of the best jobs you can get for the protection and personal value and social priority. A Commissary clerk can get contraband smuggled in and distribute it with very little risk. The merchants and middlemen of the world always become rich. If you're lucky enough to get that spot, you can retire in peace. As a cherished member of the community, and as a shared resource common to every con in the joint, the Commissary clerk enjoys a cushy existence.

No one fucks with the guy who can deny access to the postage stamps used to keep in touch with Little Mama outside in the world, while she struts before the gaze of every man who cares to look her way. No one fucks with the guy who can deny access to toothpaste and soap and deodorant and batteries. No one fucks with the guy who can deny access to ice-cream sandwiches and candy. It's not a bad way to pass the time.

The clerk on duty passes the key to the keyboard over the counter with a neutral smile, pushing forward a clipboard to sign. Then he nods and puts the black and white queens in a collateral lockbox for safekeeping.

One hour.

Sitting on the edge of the stool, fingers banging across the keys. Sounds awful, like a broken fence flapping against a brick wall.

Perhaps a bit of tuning would help.

Marty never noticed the missing kings and queens from his chess set, occupied as he was by the sealed envelope thrust into his hands, containing the key to the Boston drug scene, the treasure map to his retirement.

Lid open, one king under the strings and the other on top like a pair of dull scissors, bending and twisting and wrenching at the highest string until it pops *twang!* and slipping the four-foot length of wire from the bridge. Winding each end around a king, securing the slippery wire with a fishing knot. Surveying the work, twanging the wire for measurement.

Sounds a little sharp.

The night before the fight, sleep comes like to a tormented baby. Dreams of dodging fists, of swinging slowly with a giveaway shriek like a gull. Dreams of being the nappy giant looking down with scorn at an old man with a bar of soap in his ragged slingshot. Dreams of sailing south across the country and riding a motorcycle over the Caribbean to a palm-tree-studded beach with no cameras and no watchtowers—just coconuts and air conditioning and a friend from another lifetime.

Lights on.

Eyes snap open.

Count.

Breath quickens.

Ears fill with the sound of a pulse and the onrush of reality. Cell doors clatter. Sleepy cursing animals shuffle out along the cellblock.

Morning.

It's never a good idea to eat right before a fight. If you take a bad shot to the belly, you can throw up and choke on a bit of orange or a tater-tot. Plus the gnawing growl reminds you of the hunt. It brings the survival alertness to the forefront. The instinct of awareness. Succeed or die.

Somebody paid someone something to have a cafeteria door remain unlocked after the breakfast Count. The halls would be abandoned for fifteen minutes, giving each fighter ample time to get into the cafeteria, have it out, and disappear before anyone got wise to the situation.

Otherwise it'd be a pisser of a lockdown, with nightsticks and pepper spray and severe long-term punishments.

Each fighter was to have one witness present in the cafeteria, and no one else. Always rules. More or less the same rules of honor agreed upon for centuries and generations. The idea being to give a logical structure to an animalistic behavior. These bare-knuckle fights can't be a surprise for either fighter, and there can't be any doubt about the stakes. Picture a sumo wrestler attacking his opponent before the bow. The height of dishonor. Just a brawl.

There would be Delany Brothers all over the surrounding areas, in the laundry room folding sheets, in the kitchen doing dishes, in the showers doing...shower things. With every step, your chances of walking away from this dwindle, like your queen just got jumped by a bishop. You can win without a queen, but it's damned tricky.

There's an old saying among chess masters. Position over submission. Arrange the battle ahead of time, or else get picked off like carrion.

Marty and his Delany counterpart waiting in the cafeteria, scooting tables against the walls out of the way, while Robinson—self-styled referee, host, promoter, and organizer—directs them.

Both representatives somber. Both cordial. Talking in businesslike tones, hushed but efficient. Standing in the middle of a rough semi-circle of cafeteria tables, awaiting their respective charges.

Slap-slap-slap-slap, trotting down the hallway, stripping to the waist. Slick with sweat, warmed up and roaring to go.

Alive.

Electricity crackles through muscles; lungs fill and empty, fill and empty; heart ticks time, speeding up or slowing down to maximize the workings of the machine.

Fists clenched.

Drop into some pushups just to keep the energy going. Kick off the Crocs they provide once a year, free of charge. Loosen up the arms; twist the torso.

Strides shorten and become bouncy; head bobs to an unheard rhythm. The championship round. Investments with high rewards always have high risks. Anything else means you're being conned. This stupid petty behavior would easily result in bankrupted Good Time, loss of privileges, bad luck with the parole board, a job in the septic system—or death in the morning. On a grubby tile floor surrounded by a herd of scarred cafeteria tables.

Expected to wait the count of two hundred to let the giant get past the hallway and inside the cafeteria. Then your turn. This is it.

At some point you have to give up. Nothing lasts forever; not strength, not resolve, not memory, not life. It's a fucked up thing the way people forget that. Impermanence. It's the only real constant. The one thing that keeps the universe alive and ticking—constant renewal. And that means death. Nature balances itself. It has to.

The fear of death is a universal truth. It's what sustains the ultimate drive toward...whatever. It can be twisted or buried, but it's discernible through whatever foundation is built on top, whispering loud and clear. Obeying that voice, that Ego whose goal is to pound out a survival in a world too complex for its comprehension, is the constant struggle. Manifest it however you choose, through drugs, violence, sex—it all comes down to the inner reptile.

So when death comes around and flips a coin, you call bullshit and lay down a deal: a life for a death. A surrender of sorts for survival, if you can call it that. Trading hell for limbo. It's all relative, right? Cut corners and live in protective exile until it blows over. And just hope to maintain a slab of sanity, despite the odds.

As it turns out, no matter how hard you've been, it's not easy to go down swinging. It's easier to give up. Beg quarter from the Devil and hope the first-class cabins aren't all filled yet. What a ride it's been, and don't let the door hit you on the way out.

A game of chess doesn't end with the death of the king. He just has no more moves—and so an adventurous mind might picture him dressing in rags and slipping a thin blade between the ribs of a guard before vanishing down a clammy secret tunnel. The game is played through whatever rules are agreed upon—tacitly or otherwise.

"This isn't a game," Marty said softly. "This is real life."

Well yeah, Marty. That *is* the game.

Footsteps.

A shadow passes over the concrete floor at the end of the hall. He's coming.

Duck back behind a stairwell.

He saunters past. He's huge. Hulking. Shoulders like a bull. Fists like knots of wood. Chin like another fist. And a head of tight curly hair like velcro, almost too high to reach with a right-cross. Uppercuts out of the question.

He moves slowly, with grace, and you can see the muscles twitching across his bare back, see the athletic bounce of his heels. A warhorse. It'd almost be a shame to see this specimen destroyed. He should be off making millions in the NFL. Or more millions faking it in the movies.

But maybe he's too exaggerated even for that. Fucking freak. A goddamn menace to society. There's only one way to deal with mutants like this.

Padding barefoot behind him across the polished cement floor, as he heads for the unlocked cafeteria door.

Fists clench around wire-wrapped hand-carved kings, unspooling the line and holding it in a wide loop with fists raised in a loose fighting stance. He stops.

Freeze.

He sneezes and rubs his nose, and continues forward.

Trying not to tremble with adrenaline, closing the distance and leaping toward his back, swinging a silent left-hook over the giant's head so the wire drops around his shoulders, crossing at the back of his neck.

Draw tight, yank down, yank back.

He falls back, thrashing and gurgling.

Three hundred fifty pounds on an old man's diaphragm.

Presses out breath.

He fights like a hooked shark, and the wire creases his neck.

Pull tighter.

Wire breaks skin.

A gout of blood spills hot on the gray floor.

Pull.

Tighter.

Pull until his legs stop kicking.

Until his bowels and bladder release.

Until his thrashing becomes jerky and uncontrolled.

Until his head tips back and the gurgle becomes a sputter.

Until his weight is stifling, pinning, and there's no more movement. Until the wire bites into the bone in his neck and finally snaps under the tension. Until you waver, dizzy from lack of breath and adrenal overload and the stench—and pass out.

ooooo

You wake up and there's nothing. Blink, white, blink, white, blink, white. Nothing. Eyes go in and out of focus, finding no points of reference. Skin gropes around for something tangible; something hard, something soft. Something warm. Something cold. Something feeling. Ears strain—there's only breath.
In...
Out...
In...
Out...
Tongue, probing, tastes nothing new. Chapped lips, clenched teeth. Nose twitches, smelling dry. Nose, the great deceiver, knows nothing; not body odor, not the wool blanket, not recycled air, not dust. Numb already.
Glaring fluorescents, springing tears. Temperature neutral. Oh yeah.
How did you wind up in here? Was it what you just remembered? Or was it more like this:
"Gaeta, the fuck *you* want?"
"To report something."
"Something? Like what?"
The screw lifts the duty log sarcastically, a smirk on his face.
"A fight. And gang activity. A war's about to start."
He stops cold. "You serious? You're snitching?" He touches his taser. "You?"

"A motherfucker's gotta do what a motherfucker's gotta do. I'm not trying to go down in their flames. I'm trying to survive."

Explanations of the politics of the situation, the impossible odds. The stakes. Exaggerated for his benefit, expanded in apocalyptic fashion. Quitting the game to avoid the checkmate. "But I'm scared they'll know I told you."

"Listen, we can put you in protective custody until it blows over. No sweat."

"No sweat?"

"Well. You won't be murdered."

Sometimes in movies people will find themselves falling asleep and drifting through a dream purgatory, surrounded by and bathed in white, the overwhelming emptiness of mystery sitting heavily upon their confused shoulders. It always takes a while for them to figure out their circumstances. Then there's a reckoning and a recognition. This is what you've done, this is why you're here. Anguish. And then puzzling out how to get back to normal, back to the real world.

Solitary confinement is the opposite.

Here you dream to escape the same sameness that's all the same. And empty. Here you dream to escape the sensory deprivation of the unchanging. Here you dream because if you don't, you're not going to survive. You're not going to come out on the other side unscathed.

Alone with your thoughts—and what else is there?—with nothing to distract the senses, nothing to divert the flow of cognition. Nothing to limit or prevent rebirth or renewal, nothing to stop the revolution. There's nothing to say Yes or No to, nothing to focus on, nothing to experience that you haven't already.

Death seems less dull than a life already lived.

Bombarded by the same photons and particles, the same air and light, the same thoughts and memories, confined to an unreasonably tiny space—barely bigger than this body; this exclusive reminder of your own existence, nothing more than a tool to gather sensory input—and feeling numb numb numb numb numb numb numb numbing to the experience—and the walls can't contain you if you become them, if you blend your structure with theirs, if you align your vibrations.

The mind can only take so much of any one thing before it turns in on itself. The mind is used to constant change. Constant change and adaptation and growth. It wants the new. It *needs* the new in order to keep it sharp for the next challenge, the next obstacle to survival.

If there's too much of nothing, it creates its own world to live in, its own set of experiences to delve into. The room disappears. Before anything happens, there's a pause for effect. A hush. A stillness. Weightlessness.

And then here it comes. Between each dream the shutter closes once.

Your mind goes blank.

Coming soon from your favorite upstart author...

Louder Than Words

A novel
(with no verbs)

By Paul D Blumer

Eerie calm through streets suffuse with the stubborn hiss of street-sweepers and small-hours traffic-light rhythms. Here and there bundles of homeless cocoons in corners and on bus-station seats—but everything else empty. The unlikely ghostliness of between-time.

Bicycle scouts on patrols through side streets, on lookout for a police convoy, its handful of black city-busses, headlights dark under streetlight glow, with two empty school-busses for detainees, and several K9 units. Hordes of blue boys in full riot gear; elbow pads, kevlar vests, gas-masks, bandoliers of teargas and flashbangs—a teeth-armed contingent of bullies with billy clubs.

Watchers at each near intersection, verbal signal-fire system of shouts and internet feeds; while in the square, crash-course drills on legal and safe responses to police activity, a human chain ready for defense of the protest encampment.

Another hop of the police caravan.

Another burst of minute-by-minute updates.

Another interminable wait.

"Almost like intentional fraud in book-keeping. Unnecessary overtime."

Our ripple of quiet laughter at the not-quite joke.

Stacks of empty pizza boxes, testament to the generosity of local businesses in response to confiscation of our butane stoves. Fire hazards and violation of something-or-other. Overwhelming optimism in the air, that long-buried feeling of the goodness of things, restoration of faith in fellow man.

Word games on the sidelines, pockets of students at their books, an aging raconteur from the old days, from before the web.

"So much communication now. Internet in the sixties? My god, if only."

Update checks.

Cops at Main. No action. #peoplesprotest.

Ready every1? Legal hotline in marker on your skin? #peoplesprotest.

Safety and peace to all my brothers and sisters @peoplesprotest.

"Maybe not tonight. Too strong for them."

We. Legion.

"Or maybe an attrition strategy? A wolf cry? Until too sleepy?"

Shrugs all around.

A guy with a guitar in methodical movement through the lines, jug of cider vinegar ready for anyone in need.

For teargas.

Intimate intellectual discussions on civic rights and effective responses to police interaction. A few in a huddle over drafts of resolutions to City Council, and manifestos—too strong?—for inspiration of the rest of the world.

Vocal communication relays, sentence-by-sentence echoes for dissemination of information over noise and distance, in preparation for pandemonium. Majority inexperience and uneasy energy, with stolid support from a precious framework of reliable information holders and practical knowledge sharers.

Updates:

Caravan on the move! @peoplesprotest warning warning!

Caravan in idle along 3rd #peoplesprotest.

On the move, on the move! Cameras up, masks on @peoplesprotest.

5 blocks. On their tails, on the way back @peoplesprotest

Message circulation. Around the world, eyes wide, video feeds on and busy.

Sickening *whupwhupwhup* of helicopters, spotlights heavy; splashes of incandescent oppression, a rip through the face of civil reality.

Castoff board games, chain of elbows around the medical tent, a double line across the street. Our street.

"Peacefully!"

"Our right to *peaceful* protests."

"The cops, our brothers. Just people, like us"

Words of wisdom, words of comfort and reassurance, words of sweet bravado. Overhead, *whupwhupwhup* of helicopters, ravens over the battlefield, ready for the bloody pickings, ready for death.

"No profanity! Not our reason, not our way."

Bottles of vinegar from hand to hand, generous splashes on bandanas and particle dust masks, desperate attempts at teargas safety. Tang of vinegar over dull richness of excrement, of porta-potty chemicals, and the smolder of body odor and stale tents.

A siren *whoop.*

First flashes of blue lights around a corner.

The caravan.

Whupwhupwhup.

City block of menace, vehicles slow through the night. Wary of booby traps.

A halt for dismount. Flood of on-foot police, in loose formation with shields low and weapons lower, for now. Still distant, with diesel engines in reserve.

Sirens.

"Enough!" the scream of a veteran in utility duds, open across his chest, heavy with medals. "These civilians;" his hoarse cry, on camera for the world. "Why violence? Against peaceful protesters? Against your brothers and sisters, citizens like you, of *this country!*" Indignation in waves, infectious energy and passion, the strength of experience and service. "Fundamental human rights," tension in his finger against his chest, indignant and on simmer. "Service and protection." We, in orbit around his gravity, an echo of his words. "Pro-teck-shun," his bitter reinforcement.

Siren *whoop.*

In continuous unison, rustle of uniforms and clack of high-impact plastic. Boots on asphalt, a slow stamp toward protesters with signs on strings, after official carry-stick bans for our safety.

Down the street, a lava flow of formation, a broad strip of pavement between two armies.

Night breeze through tarps and makeshift shelters, constant targets of police action. No camps in public places. No overnight freedom of assembly.

Phalanx of fearful but steady citizens, weaponless against the imminent onslaught. Students arm-in-arm with vagrants arm-in-arm with single mothers arm-in-arm with overqualified and underemployed youth arm-in-arm with nine-to-fivers with work-ready alarm clocks in empty bedrooms.

Faceless uniforms, an array of deliberate movements, safe behind masks and helmets, badges and orders. The thug fist of oligarchy.

Song from the people's midst, a single clear voice of peace and togetherness, a slightly off-key ballad, stark against the coppery fear of the unarmed many against the murder-sanctioned few.

A halt.

"CITIZENS IN OCCUPATION OF THE AREA WITHIN JURISDICTION OF SECTION 409, PUBLIC PLAZAS. AFTER EIGHT PM, REMAINDER IN THE AREA, REGARDLESS OF PURPOSE—A VIOLATION. TO YOUR HOMES, PLEASE."

Our grim reply: "Whose streets?"

Our streets.

Whose streets?

Our streets!

Deployment. Solid living machine against defiant human wall. Eyes across no-man's-land, a meeting of resolve, grim realization of humanity on both sides, distinct only because of uniform and paycheck, and divine directive of control.

Supportive voices, with love even for cops, hopeful still for peace.

"You, the people! Cops the people too!"

"Service and protection. Please!"

"Your pensions and benefits also empty! Same team, same team."

Martial orders.

A stir of resolve; tension through the crowd.

Thoonk! slow arc of smoke, clatter of steel on pavement, hiss of CS gas.

Bated breath. Hovering silence.

Whupwhupwhup overhead.

Blast of spotlights behind silhouette lines of apocalyptic troops.

Whose streets?

OUR streets!

"EVERYBODY OUT. CITIZENS TO YOUR HOMES," the bullhorn still agrowl, still hopeful; woeful misestimation of resolve. Service and protection of the rich and powerful, ignorant of the plight in the trenches.

Whose streets?

Our streets!

Video cameras and smartphones up high, all manner of signs in air.

A slipper in the streetlight, narrow no-man's-land of concrete and road paint; just inches apart, human chain and riot shields. Sneakers toe-to-toe with boots.

"Peacefully!" screams from calm intellectuals and laid-off teachers. "No violence."

"Same boat, us and them! Please, peacefully, everybody."

A banner overhead: *Police: pink slips away from The People.*

Behind the human chain, by the kitchen tent, an angry few with bricks, ready for hand-to-hand defense of our right to peaceful assembly.

Official surge forward, clear plastic human battering ram fifty wide and ten deep.

Thoonk! of teargas canisters, hot spirals at citizens' feet.

Eyes wide, we the people under headlight glare. We the defaced masses, in frozen terror and rigid refusal against the ire of the system. Churn of individuals elbow-in-elbow, a sum greater than its parts, headlong into chaos. Uniforms and nightsticks against indignation and terror.

Whupwhupwhup overhead, blast of spotlights, red glow of flares.

A mantle of smoke, sounds of gags, coughs, sobs. Poisonous glow of streetlights. Shrieks and whistles, chants and songs, air thick with cordite and the alien heat of volatile aerosol powder.

From the protesters, plastic cups of paint, yellow and red, in vivid arcs toward the cops. Splashes of color, artistry against the State's monochromatic oppression.

Clatter of telescope batons, the push of protection and service, the jostle, the struggle for balance, arm-in-arm, jaws tight. Our chain still strong.

Thoonk! of teargas canisters, *whupwhupwhup* of helicopters, tears in red eyes, vinegary bandanas over faces, the press of riot shields. Volunteer medics at the ready, shades of doubt. On one side, grim whiteshirts with radios and scowls, and on the other, a congregation of hecklers and chanters.

"Shame! Shame! Shame!"
"Ze good Germans!"
"Love for po-lice!"
Equal force along the line, advancement and resistance in neutral.
Another sharp order.
And then the batons.

Title and content subject to change.
For more information, please see the author's website at:
www.paulblumer.com

Made in the USA
Lexington, KY
04 March 2013